PRAISE FOR *SISTE*

Revenge, persecution, loneliness, the need for community and love and companionship, our fear of the other—all are woven in a tale that begins with an epic battle and ends with a tender moment of peace.

– Sherry Roberts, author of *Crow Calling*, *Book of Mercy* and *Maud's House*

In this vividly imagined world, readers gain a new perspective on *Beowulf*. Through the eyes of a monster's sister, we explore the richness of an epic's margins, the nature of generosity, and what one generation owes the next.

– Kim Todd, author of *Sensational, The Hidden History of America's*
Girl Stunt Reporters

If you like lush writing, stories of female heroism, and the fight for survival, then Susan Thurston's *Sister of Grendel* is the book for you.

– Judith Yates Borger, author of *Where's Billie?*, *Whose Hand?* and *Who Bombed the Train?*

I was especially taken by the deeply spiritual and erotic romance Thurston weaves into the narrative. The references to the foods, herbs, and plants throughout the story... are sumptuous details that added to the pleasurable experience of reading this novel. What a sensual feast.

– Cynthia Uhrich, award-winning filmmaker and co-author of *My Life in the Purple Kingdom*

The story's layered and well-developed characters, combined with the tension, twists and sensory and poetic descriptions, hooked me from the beginning and held me to end.

– Therese Pautz, author of *Raven Creek* and *Rain and Revelation*

Sister of Grendel is a marvel of storytelling, as well as a haunting miracle of reimagination of every preconception not just of *Beowulf*, but of the possibilities of fiction. For 1,000 years over 3,000 lines, this epic poem has been wrung through every possible interpretation except this one: Grendel, perhaps not as monstrous as legend has it, is accompanied this time by a sibling, at times his conscience, protector, apologist, critic, and even occasional victim. Astonishing in its originality, one ultimately can only repeat the final words of the fictional interlocuter that transmutes the tale: "I whispered," she says of Rehsotis, Grendel's sister, "I will never forget you."

– Neal Karlen, contributor to the *New York Times*, author of *This Thing Called Life*, a biography/memoir of Prince.

SISTER OF GRENDEL

**CALUMET
EDITIONS**
Minneapolis

First Edition July 2022
Sister of Grendel. Copyright © 2022 by Susan Thurston.
All rights reserved.

This is a work of fiction. All of the characters, names, incidents, organizations, and dialogue are either the products of the author's imagination or are used fictitiously.

Printed in the United States of America.
10 9 8 7 6 5 4 3 2 1

ISBN: 978-1-950743-88-9

Cover and book design by Gary Lindberg

SISTER OF GRENDEL

SUSAN THURSTON

**CALUMET
EDITIONS**
Minneapolis

For my children
Madeleine and Samuel

CONTENTS

ALSO BY SUSAN THURSTON

Anthologies

Low Down, Coming On

Open to Interpretation: Water's Edge

Penchant

Tremors Vibrations Enough to Rearrange the World

Upon Arrival of Illness: Coming to Terms with the Dark Companion

Culinary

Cooking Up the Good Life with Chef Jenny Breen

Poetry

Wild Bone Season (Chapbook)

PREFACE

Decades ago, when I first read *Beowulf,* my sympathies aligned not with the Geats or the titular mercenary, but with the invaded: Grendel and his mother. Time passed. I read new translations and re-imaginings and re-read familiar versions. My sympathies did not waiver. And in the blurred and misty hours of caring for my infant son, I was visited by a voice of another. Her words were clear: "There was a sister." She wanted to tell her story. I listened. She gave me her name. And during the intervening years, I transcribed her words of a time before, during, and after the legend. My son is now a tall young man. Some stories take ages to tell.

PROLOGUE

The two of you flee. You move toward a safer life—mother and daughter. He does not follow you. I have seen to that.

Sequestered in my forest-secluded den, with these sheets of paper, this pen and ink, I will write my story. This is my final ritual of closure. Here I chronicle my life.

I do not have much time. Darkness thickens around and within me. Change in my body is pronounced and sudden. I no longer wander or run with wolves. I cannot swim for days in clear lakes. All changes. The wolves, who consider me a curious ally in their hunt, sniff at my doorway, hoping I will join them. The old gray one with the white ears is the matriarch who watches me as I take a step toward them. She sniffs my hand and understands my pain. With a moaned farewell, she leads the pack away. Later, I hear their howling praises to the moon. I watch their shadows dance among the birch and long to be with them. I fall into a burdened sleep. In my dreamscape I am young. I gather food in the forest with the elders, run to the sea with my brother, listen to my mother's songs, dance through our sacred Labyrinth. Then I see my brother Grendel in fierce struggle with his killer Beowulf. I awake screaming.

Exhausted and weeping, I stagger to the stream for water. I am careless with my fire, and too often it nearly burns out. From my larder

I take fennel seeds and deer marrow, grind them into a rich paste that I eat with my fingers. Its nuttiness clears my head; my aching joints ease.

I will keep writing.

I am the last of my kind.

I am the only one who remains of the tribe of Anath—the long-lived.

My name is Rehsotis.

Sister of Grendel.

PART ONE

LABYRINTH

My earliest memories are the certainty of an elder's embrace, the honeyed tingle of summer mead, a bleeding spread of sunrise.

My mother is called Yenheth. She stands taller than anyone else, with a lean muscular strength that speaks of protection. The others in the tribe remark that I favor her. Sun burnishes her skin and her amber hair glistens long down her back. Glittering bright amber stones on brass loops dance from her long-lobed ears. In her eyes I see the sky. She breathes in the evening air as if it were a delicacy she can taste. I admire her long and thin nose, her high cheekbones, and the way she moves as if she were made of water. Running, her exquisite feet seem made of delicate sinew. When she speaks, she gestures with her hands, and they skim and dance in the air like elegant, pale birds.

I climb into her arms and frame her face between my hands. I search for my reflection in her eyes. "Oh, you are the most beautiful thing in the world," I say.

"Daughter Rehsotis," she says, "you know so little of the world. Beautiful? Ah…no, no. Your great-grandmother, she was beautiful."

* * *

Other tribes have their temples and hold them dear. We have our Labyrinth.

"Hear how the Labyrinth came to be," says my mother Yenheth. She drapes her robe around her shoulders and settles against warm cushions, fending off the chill night air, then turns and nods toward my brother Grendel and me.

"Your great-grandmother Chanan dreams of a path through the forest. She follows it to a place where a brilliant light flows like water. The water turns from azure to amber, from amber to emerald. It washes over her, carries her to different lands where she moves among other people and encounters unfamiliar creatures. When she awakens, she keeps her eyes closed, and in her dream memory, makes her way to the edge of the forest. Then she opens her eyes and discovers she has found the path, just as in her dream. The path leads her into the darkest part of the forest; she is not afraid and keeps moving deeper into the woods. At last she comes upon a clutch of tamarack trees encircling several large boulders. She leans against one of the rocks, and the elegant trees' branches begin to glow, the needle-thin leaves flicker. The light illuminates outlines on the rock—hundreds of engraved pictures and inscriptions.

"The rocks crack and fall apart around her. She cannot breathe. Cannot cry out. Music of reeds and drums fills the air and vibrates through her body until she thinks of nothing but the music—until she is the music. And in the seams of the sounds, she sees images from the future, of things yet to be. Lights swirl and flow over her, into her through her nose, mouth, ears. The light at first tastes sweet as honey, then sour as vinegar, and she becomes ill from its potency. The lights flare out. She is lifted into the air and then dashed to the ground within.

"The tamarack trees have burned to the ground and the uneven stones still bear their engravings. Chanan carries each stone into the village and fits them together. She refuses help from anyone."

It is here in the telling that Grendel and I nestle close to our mother Yenheth. She strokes our foreheads and chants the rest of the tale, and we join her in reciting the familiar words until the night air thrums.

> Stone by stone, the Labyrinth.
> Stone by stone it is set.
> See the beasts and flying creatures.
> Anathians dancing, singing—
> Some alone, some together.
> Each envisions as is met
> When one enters the Labyrinth of Chanan
> Take its message
> And well consider, it is well meant.
> Be it blessing, warning, other?

* * *

The spring day is glorious in promise. Grendel and I are young, and we leave our duties in the gardens to spend time in the Labyrinth.

We race each other to the entrance, and Grendel dashes ahead of me calling back to me over his shoulder, "Just try to keep up with me! See, Sister, I am stronger and faster than you!"

"You are not," I shriek as I run after him and into the Labyrinth. As always, the engraved images enthrall me more than any youthful game. Soon I stop listening for Grendel's footfall and do not care if I catch up to him. Instead, I lean into the sounds the Labyrinth offers. I find myself held by a stone on which the figures become the leaves and branches of a tree, softening and turning, flush with color, and I am wrapped and rocked gently within the now-pulsing limbs. I close my eyes and drift into a soft slumber.

When I awake, I find myself stretched out along the base of the wall at a corner. The sun is warm and it is quiet. I complete my journey into the Labyrinth's center, make my way back out, and do not encounter Grendel. I assume he simply did not want to disturb me while I was resting and passed by me on his way out.

We meet again at our evening meal. I expect him to tease me about having failed to catch him in the Labyrinth. But he is silent and brooding over his bread and cheese.

I think nothing more about it.

Days later Grendel and I walk through the settlement and come near the Labyrinth's entrance.

"Try to catch me this time, Grendel. I shall show you who is truly swifter and stronger," I shout as I dash toward the portal.

Grendel stands fixed at the Labyrinth's entrance and cries out to me, "Rehsotis, please come back! Don't make me follow you there."

"I am here!" I stop just before the first turn in the wall. "Come and seek me. Do not be afraid."

"I am not afraid," he bellows. "But the rocks are so dark. The creatures, they want to devour me. They have begun to say horrible things to me."

"Dark? It is midday, Grendel! The Labyrinth will not harm you. Come in. Come toward me. The voices from the stones are not malevolent. Their images are well fit and made. Nothing will harm you."

"No." Grendel bolts toward me to catch me into his arms and prevent me from going any farther. "They are waiting for me. They shift and move, following me, hating me."

I look into his eyes and see terror there. "What is it? What happened to you?"

We lean against each other and lurch out of the Labyrinth. I guide him to a sycamore tree where he collapses, trembling in my arms. "The last time I came into the Labyrinth, I saw things," he whispers.

"We all do. That is part of the power."

"No. This was different. The creatures—the creatures of the walls, they told me what would become of me, and it was—they were…" He presses his head into my shoulder and lets me hold him. I try to comfort him with tender strokes and soft song at his ear. Then he hears our mother Yenheth calling for him, pushes away, leaves me alone with my confusion.

* * *

The Time of Thirst changes everything for everyone in the valley. The rain does not come in winter. It does not come in the spring. Pomegranates and olives wither on their branches. Deer and boar roam and rummage farther away to find food. We turn increasingly to our storehouses.

The Smallheaded live in greater numbers in the valley. They do not temper their consumption, even as food sources dwindle. Increasingly, the Smallheaded lift hands and fists against us over who will gather the shriveling olives from the grove or the diminishing clusters of red grapes from the vines. After each encounter, Yenheth calls the elders together and they select an ambassador who is sent to the Smallheaded's settlement to arrive at a strained agreement: We will share, we will conserve, and we will make our way through this time of want in concert. Again and again, an agreement is set. Again and again, a Smallheaded hunter or gatherer breaks the pact.

* * *

In the middle of a steaming summer night, while cicadas thrum the dry air, the Smallheaded come, casting oversized shadows in the torchlight. They ransack the storehouse. They bludgeon to death our guard, leave him nearly unrecognizable.

In the morning Yenheth mounts the archway, marking the entrance to the Labyrinth, and shouts, "I cannot fathom your cowardice. Decades ago, we should have wiped this world clean of the Smallheaded. It would have been so easy when they did not outnumber us by so many. Our tolerance has led to this. Now one of our own is murdered. It is time to face this struggle squarely."

Again the elders gather, and after a long deliberation through the day and into night, Yenheth announces that despite her disapproval, the Tribe of Anath will abandon the valley.

"And what of our Labyrinth?" I stand next to Grendel and he takes my hand when I ask the question.

Yenheth turns to the two of us standing shoulder-to-shoulder, but her eyes do not meet mine. "We cannot take it with us. It is too great a burden."

"But that cannot be." Now Yenheth looks at me. "It has been at the center of our lives for centuries. We are already abandoning our homes. Must we also abandon what has been the touchstone of our souls?"

"Rehsotis." She inhales and seems to hold her breath before continuing. "We are not in numbers large enough to move it—even with our charms."

"Then at least the archway. Let us at least carry that with us."

Grendel does not hesitate. "Yes. Let us do that, Mother. I will help her. We two will be caretakers of those stones."

Yenheth turns to look at the Labyrinth.

I measure my words. "At least a part. That is all. And when we come to our next home, it will be a symbol for us all."

And then she is nodding. "Very well."

We roll up our tapestries, pack our instruments. Grendel and I dismantle the entrance stones of the Labyrinth. We fit our goats with sturdy carts and pack them with their precious load. By the light of the full moon, we depart. We head north, in the direction Yenheth dreams we will find a place without the Smallheaded, where we will live and thrive in peace.

* * *

After many moons of trudging, we arrive on the shores of the North Sea, where there are no Smallheaded. In an even clearing near woodland and not far from the shore, we erect the arch of the Labyrinth and reconstruct our lives. We are left to ourselves for season upon season and begin to believe it will always be so. We build dwellings with tight, hive-shaped vaults from stone blocks quarried from the nearby cliffs. Into entryway lintels we carve intricate designs, with the most elaborate created for our large common hall. The soil is loamy and rich, and in our gardens we grow greens, beans, and root vegetables with plenty to preserve. We lay up stores of seeds, mead, and pickled fruits. From reeds and grasses we weave baskets. We hunt and trap the deer and boar that roam languidly through the forest and along the shoreline; we tan their hides into soft robes, dry every scrap of their meat, and turn their bones into tools and embellishments for our dwellings. The forest offers amber-grained wood, from which we make instruments and capacious chairs. We find ore crumbling from a nearby gorge, and we forge tools, elegant buckles, and palm-fitting goblets.

This is the Golden Age for the Tribe of Anath. The stone workers erect an Arch of Blessing at the eastern edge of our settlement, through which we pass to gather food from the woodland or the sea. We cultivate gardens of colorful beans, sweet cucurbits, and fragrant herbs. Around the heart of the settlement, we erect a circle of stones at the precise points to mark the seasons, moon shifts, and position of the stars.

* * *

Grendel masters whatever interests him. And as soon as he attains an accomplished level of skill, he moves on to something else. He leans against the knee of the herdsman as he milks the goats or curries the soft hair from their bellies; he duplicates the process with ease. He perfects custardy oaken cheeses. After only one lesson, he twists strong and even yarn from a spindle. His strength increases during time spent at the forge, and with a heavy mallet and expert twists and pulls of the metal, he fashions precisely balanced tools embellished with patterns intricate as lace. He works with the gardeners, and for several lush seasons he pulls weeds, sets seedlings into cultivated beds, and shapes the vines into graceful long-armed sentries along the fence lines.

One late summer, Grendel strides up to me, carrying a bowl heaped with egg-shaped, emerald-fleshed fruit.

"Here. Try. I have just picked it from my trees. Their first season to bear fruit." He hands me one and his eyes twinkle.

Years ago when he grafted two varieties of fruit together, he suffered the gibes from mother: "What are you thinking? The stems will both die or one will overtake the other. Perfect the best of the young saplings and do not waste effort."

I take the fruit while watching his face, wondering if I am a victim of some joke. The warm, tender flesh gushes with the flavor of pomegranate and black currant. Beneath green skin, the fruit is the vivid claret of pomegranate with the consistency of apricot, and at the heart a syrupy dumpling of chewy seeds.

After this triumph in the orchard, Grendel's interest shifts yet again. In sequence, he spends time with the weavers, masons, and bakers. With devoted passion, he watches their every move, works at their side, and soon surpasses their own skill. He cycles through each art or craft practiced by the tribe, and his prodigious, albeit fickle, talent brings showers of praise.

* * *

During my search for my best role, there are not so many successes. My attempts at mead-making lead to cloudy, stinky disasters. My temper pumps like the bellows when I try to work metal. My hands turn the glossy sage and oak-colored threads set for a carpet into a colorful imbroglio.

But when I sit within the circle of tribe members stringing a lute or buffing the pear-shaped body of a rebec, I know I have found my place. When I take a piece of wood into my hands, I sense the seasons the tree has known—times of abundance, years of constant thirst, prevailing twists of wind, or an unexpected skewer of lightning. As I work the wood, various tones and colors ripple before my eyes. I blend and mingle the strips of wood and favor forest catheus—along the bridge, behind the fingerboard, within the neck or over the lower bout with whorled artistry. Each player takes up one of my string boxes, rests it under her chin or across her lap, and draws a tight bow over its stretched gut strings, and *knows* me. With one of my creations, one never plays alone.

* * *

In a golden autumn, when we are busy filling vessels with mead and milled seeds, a tribe we call the Wanderers settle near us. We are cautious with them for some time, concerned they will be like the other Smallheaded. They trade stories, songs, and rolls of azure and russet-colored silks for our handcrafted goods. They love my instruments, and in time, each of them has several. Many full moon nights are spent together singing and feasting. All our voices join and thread together within the layers of vibrating strings, cool reeds, and taut rhythms of our instruments. When the instruments and our voices blend in star-glittered perfection, the air thickens with the flavor of rosebuds and pepper.

One of the Wanderers seeks me out and we share honey-drizzled days. She is an older woman, dark skinned like the others, but with seafoam blue eyes instead of dark brown. Her cheeks look like dried plums; her hair is thick and falls in white-streaked locks to her knees. We spend hours playing soulful duets with my lutes and lyre, and she talks about all she has seen.

"I will die soon," she tells me one evening when the western sky is streaked thick with orange and magenta. "And when I die, I will be buried deep, standing up, facing the direction from which we all came."

"Yes. My kind. Your kind. Even the others who do not understand us and our ways. We all came from the south now, you know that. You are even older than I, so certainly you know this."

I nod. "How it is that we come from the same place, drink from the same wells, sleep beneath the same sky, and yet we turn against each other?"

"We are not against each other." She draws her red cloak tighter around her shoulders.

"Ah. Yes. They are not willing to comprehend any more than what serves them. They want to claim all before them as their own— land, fauna, flora, other people. They want to have charge over it all, prescribe how we do what we already know. That is why we keep moving. We are not willing to bend to their will," she says.

"It is because of the Smallheaded that we moved here," I say.

She sighs. "And they will keep forcing you to move on, unless and until you are ready to make a stand."

When she smiles, her gray teeth gleam like uneven freshwater pearls. I shiver.

The red-plumed sun settles deep into her nest and we sit in silence until it is dar, and the communal fires burn strong several strides away from us. We hear the others making music, their bodies thrown into dark silhouettes by the firelight. In such dark, it is difficult to distinguish Anathian from Wanderer.

That night, my friend of the Wanderers dies in her sleep.

We take turns digging a deep narrow pit in the soft earth. After binding her straight and stiff up to her neck in a colorful winding sheet, her daughter and son lower her into the pit. She faces south. As she wished. As is their custom.

The Wanderers take her death as a sign that it is time for them to move on. The night before they leave, they come to our village and trade for some seeds, dried fruit, and all of my unclaimed instruments —even those I haven't yet strung. In return, I accept soft leather pouches of mixed and powerful herbs, small boxes filled with glittering flaked and powdered dyes gathered during their travels through distant lands, and elaborate bands and brooches of metal spun and braided as if made of gold and silver spider web.

* * *

Many years after the Wanderers leave, another band of the Smallheaded appear. They are few in number, and not as strong or fierce as others, so we believe that this time we can coexist. Some of the elders go to speak with them and return believing we have an understanding. We exchange goods. Sometimes, in the dead of winter, their leaders gather with us around our great fire in the central hall. We try to share stories, but the rhythm of laughter and good humor finds no place among us.

As seasons pass, others join their group, arriving in long and keen ships. No longer do they offer to trade portions of what they gather and grow in their gardens for our goods, crafts, or surplus food. As their numbers increase, they spend less time with us until they do not even acknowledge us if we pass each other on the pathways to the forest or to the shoreline.

In the harbor they build well-timbered docks. With the supplies they haul into the harbor on their boats and gather from the land, they erect a large hall of wood beams and yellow stone. It takes more than a year to build it, rising without beauty upon a hillside. The hall's purpose is clear: division and defense.

One night, several of the most brutish and vulgar of their lot come to our settlement, drunk upon their mead, carrying torches and lifting their loud voices. We watch from narrow openings at our dwellings' doorways as they swagger into our midst, leaning against each other and shouting, "You are the spawn of Cain. Vermin from dark lands. We do not want you here."

They howl and scream, throw their heads back and bay at the moon like jackals. They try to set fire to some of our dwellings, but inside our thick walls we chant our most potent spells of protection, and the flames do not take.

"What? See! The fire does not consume," one of the Smallheaded shrieks. "You are all from the devil. You must leave or you will be forced to leave. Demons depart. Demons depart."

The others join in his call as they run from us. In the torchlight, their eyes glitter red.

The next morning Yenheth and the elders gather. Again, most of the elders argue that it is time to leave. Yenheth refuses to hear of it; she urges them to stay, that this time we should fight the Smallheaded. Grendel and I hover outside the central hall of our family dwelling while she argues fiercely with the elders for hours that become days. Sometimes Yenheth allows us inside, but only to deliver food and drink. One night the loud voices soften and fold into murmurs. Then the elders file out behind Yenheth, and all of us gather close around my mother at our communal fire.

"Hear our agreement," she calls. "We shall leave, but we shall also stay and fight. Instead of moving on, we will move within."

She nods when she sees confused glances and scattered whispers. "Within the earth. Below where you stand. We shall not run, but we shall move into the many-chambered heart of sea caverns along our shore just north of the calm harbor. There we shall wait, bide our time, and plan to reclaim what is ours."

"Wait? Wait and plan? For what and for how much time?" Grendel asks.

"We will gather all we can. Only the archway of the Labyrinth will be taken apart and brought with us. The rest of the settlement we will abandon. After we have prepared our new home, under the cover of darkness we will walk through the entry Arch of Blessing and go to the sea. The Smallheaded will think we have left in resignation. They will wonder where we have gone. Then they will start to forget their worries, and just when they begin to believe we have left forever, then we will become ghosts. We will haunt them—enter their dreams. And they shall fear us. They shall depart in terror and our land will be restored to us."

* * *

And so, we prepare for our transition into the caverns that open and turn into the cliffs along the sea like empty honeycomb chambers. From evening until early dawn, while the Smallheaded close themselves tight within their fortification, we carry tools, food, and most of our other belongings down into these caverns, and along with our burdens, we carry even more abundant hopes. Some of us begin "to live below," as we call it, and with the flint of our fire kits, the edge of our tools, and the beauty of our spirit, we turn those glittering crystal-covered, high-vaulted and echoing interiors into our new temple. We carve shelves and columns, porticos and curved seats into the walls. Sage and applewood fires scrub some of the chill and damp from the air. We suspend and mount heavy carpets and dense tapestries from the walls and along thick beams, dividing the large dens into smaller and warmer places.

Within the farthest chamber, we reassemble the Labyrinth. Far above in the domed stone, a deep fissure lets in enough sun to suffuse the space in a green light during the day. We turn a central chamber into our gathering place, in the middle of which we build a large fire. It is banked each night and tended constantly each day.

After several full moons, the caverns are ready. In the darkest night, we walk away from our previous lives and descend into our future. During the day, we work at keeping some fashion of our old rhythms. Only at night do we emerge to hunt and gather essentials such as peat, wood, wild onions, or sorrel. All of us ache for sunlight. We want to believe we will surmount this time of asylum, and moreover, transcend it.

Our most gifted dream-gliders enter the night dramas of the Smallheaded and torment them with nightmares of agony and horror. The Smallheaded awaken in cold sweats, shaken by the power of the lingering dream images, and in the daylight they gather around our abandoned settlement and tell each other, "See… nothing but dreams. They are gone. Gone like shadows and illusions, without power or substance."

Seasons pass and the Smallheaded remain, and we continue our secret existence and increase the plague of foul dreams, yet their numbers grow. To protect themselves from their night fears seeded by our dream-gliding, they erect more dwellings outside their castle wall. Within its circle, they build an enormous stone hall with entranceway and window lintels embellished with braided patterns, and rooftops crowned by a thick wooden tower carved in the shape of a long-toothed dragon. When we present ourselves as shadows who moan warnings and threats about how they will be punished for their ill-treatment of the Tribe of Anath, they do not budge but add stone to the thickness of their walls.

My mother Yenheth's predictions do not come to bear.

One evening, one of our hunters creeps to the surface too early, carelessly impatient for darkness. Just as she is about to snatch a sleeping hare from its nest, a band of the Smallheaded descend upon her. Despite her strength and prowess, she proves no match for the group, armed as they are with clubs and daggers. They leave her for dead near the cliffs. Grendel finds her mangled body as he begins his own hunt in the night, and he carries her tenderly back into our midst.

Grendel tells us that he overheard the Smallheaded. "They say they think she was alone, that we left her behind because they cannot find any traces of the rest of us. And they believe a wolf or some other creature carried her body away."

The elders argue for Yenheth to let the attack pass, that more harm will come if we strike back without a well-considered plan. But the attack has enraged her, and she calls for retribution.

In Grendel she finds her greatest ally. His nature absorbs her increasing rage, and his hatred for the Smallheaded fills her with a twisted delight. We live in a state of uncertainty. Grendel begins to spend most of his time above ground. He is secretive and gifted at observing and watching the Smallheaded without leaving any trace. Yet they can feel his nearness. He laughs as they turn and look over their shoulders, their steps hurried as they move from errands in the woods back to the safety of their walled settlement.

"They are vigilant and have added guards around their walls," Grendel tells us. "And they keep trying to reassure each other that she did not disappear through magic. But I sense they do not completely believe their own stories about what happened to our huntress."

Grendel buries his head in Yenheth's lap and rants against the Smallheaded. She strokes his large brow with her long fingers and murmurs comforts, gentle urgings in soft, indistinct whispers. She nurtures the murderous yearnings rising in his young heart.

* * *

Under the cover of darkness and the strength of his own incantation that renders him unseen, Grendel goes into the midst of the Smallheaded to observe their habits. He returns to us and talks about observing them during their evening rituals.

"They call themselves Scyldings. There is one they call Hrothgar. They do his bidding. I do not understand why, for he offers them no tales worthy of retelling," says Grendel. "He leaves the story-weaving to others upon whom he calls. Their songs are tuneless and their voices drone like wasps. Listen." And he recreates one of the songs he heard. We cover our ears and wince. Grendel laughs. "You agree? Wasps. Mindless, droning wasps who chew upon good things and then spit it all back out upon themselves. They call that stack of stone and wood Heorot Hall. Crude and lacking any grace. As my mother Yenheth has said, 'What is built reflects the builder.' All we need to know about these Smallheaded is clear."

* * *

Beneath a full moon, I come upon Grendel, standing at the edge of the sea cliff. At his feet is a body, and in the moonlight, I can see that his robes are covered in blood. Grendel turns to look at me, then looks down at the lifeless creature and kicks it with his foot. He reaches down and with a shout, grasps the man's arm and twists it at the shoulder until it snaps, pulling it off as if he were easily tearing into a roasted rabbit. He does the same to the other arm. He lifts his blade above his head and brings it down upon the man's neck again and again until he severs the head from the torso. Gasping, he drops the sword and tosses the arms, the body, and then the head like scraps to a canine sycophant into the deep cove where giant sea brutes rise up, smooth and glistening, to swallow the parts with long-toothed satisfaction.

Grendel pushes past me and makes his way down along the narrow rock ledges to our sea cave. Waves crash white and constant over the breakers where sea creatures loll until dawn ridges the eastern horizon pink. I also retreat into our many-chambered cave.

I think about Grendel and weep for us both, aching with longing for the time when I would not have imagined my brother driven to such a brutal act. I weep for our lost innocence and tremble in the naked realization that we are moving into even darker shadows. I weep for what we relinquish, and for what we will never have. A bell jar of murderous recollection drops over my bed. Blood and loss instead of breath and grace.

Night after night, Grendel enters Heorot and claims another victim. Night after night, the Smallheaded Scyldings shudder and tremble, wondering who will be the next to die. When they post regular guards to stand throughout the night, Grendel slips a spell of confusion or incoherence upon them, and they cannot see him approaching. When he releases them from the spell, their horror as they discover another mangled body amuses him. Grendel's daring increases with his pride as he adds to his murder count. He plays with his victims. Sometimes he leaves behind a torn limb. Sometimes as he carries away the corpse, he purposefully trails a blood line out of the hall entrance. And when he leaves the corpse behind and the Scyldings try to light the pyre of honor beneath their fallen, Grendel casts a spell to keep the flame from catching, adding another layer of humiliation to their grief.

The constant night horrors drive their leader Hrothgar near a breaking point. We listen to Grendel's descriptions of the unrest and arguments within the rough walls of Heorot. I begin to believe the Scyldings soon will all leave, and we can begin to ascend to renewed lives in the world aboveground.

Even Hrothgar's dreams bear this out. Yenheth enters his dreams and the next morning she brings tales to us as we break our fast.

"He dreams about how to gather his kind and take them elsewhere upon their long-bodied boats. To leave us. All we needed is patience and a little more of Grendel's force applied with strategy and cunning," she tells us. Yenheth throws back her head and laughs—a music held within her for years. She cries, "I can nearly taste it, kindred. The sweetness of our future is honey upon my tongue. The future—think of it—without the scent of the Smallheaded too near us, their greedy dreams cleared from our skies."

That evening she brings out the drinking horns and calls the music makers forth. She lifts the horns, filled with honey wine, to the dream messengers in gratitude for their good news. She lifts the horns to Grendel, who makes himself ready for another night to advance her cause.

He arches his back and reaches out as if to embrace all of us at once, and stands resplendent in the blue robes of the royal line, his shoulders draped and gleaming with the large cowls stitched from iridescent skins.

Yenheth calls for even more music, and we each take from our personal chests and cabinets our long-silent lutes, drums, song boxes, and reeds. Sometimes, in the last few years, when our hearts could not bear any more of the longing, one or another of us would steal away with our chosen instrument to a distant corner and play long-loved and heart-remembered tunes. But we have not played together for many seasons, and we all eagerly respond to the call to gather in song.

"The Smallheaded have wrested away too much of what brought us unity. I was wrong to not let us gather and make our songs all this time. Music-tellers, bring forth your magic. Tonight, we conjure our ancestors' spirits and shape the air with our jubilation," Mother calls.

We stack armfuls of peat logs upon the communal fire and set lit torches like burning sprays of flowers throughout the hive-domed chamber. Arms linked, we dance. Voices braid into layered tones and variations of old stories and lilting calls. Everyone eats roasted nuts and roots from sweetgrass baskets. Some of us bring out thick rounds of fragrant cheese from their cool, moss-lined nests. Others take fish fresh from the evening's catch, wrap it in strips of deer fat and leaves of sage, and set it to roast and steam above the fire. We pour mead and wine from storeroom amphorae into our polished cups and drink with relish. We are warm with anticipation, our fears now smooth and quiet as a tide pool. No one notices as Grendel slips away from us.

And when Grendel returns, what does he see? What does he find, but the several dozen of us who endure, the sum and total of the once proud and strong Tribe of Anath, still making music, dancing, regaining the rhythm of an ancient race? We are certainly a beautiful vision, and with a deep-throated glad-hearted roar he calls us to attention. He stands dripping with saltwater at the chamber's entrance. This time Grendel carries his victim's body like a mantel around his shoulders. He shoulders a warrior whose great eyes are fixed open by death — the boar-shaped helmet still on his head. His mouth is twisted in the silenced scream of one awakened abruptly and snuffed amid a mead-clouded sleep.

Grendel stands before us, chest broad and soaked with blood, eyes glittering and terrifying. He does not only catch the light from the torches but seems to emit a fire of his own, fueled by an awareness of his power and his sense of what is nearly at hand. He appears glorious and exquisite. And ultimately so sad. I find myself weeping in the midst of the tribal warmth that grows around all of us. This is the flush of victory, and within it, I taste my own fear. I cannot find the words for my foreboding. Certainly not the words any of my tribe folk want to hear.

Instead, I cross to Grendel and lift the Smallheaded's dead body from my brother's shoulders. The others fall silent as they watch me stretch the corpse out at his feet. Then I take my brother into my arms and call to a different Grendel, the one I knew and loved from our childhood. "Brother, certainly you feel glorious, but you are not like this. We are not like this. This cannot and will not end well. Look around you. We are too few. We have been driven beneath all of creation for too long."

He pushes me away and does not look me in the eye. "Do you have a different solution? A better way?" He does not address me alone, but everyone gathered around us.

"We walk an unnatural and unsavory path, and even if it is one foisted upon us, if we continue on it, we will find ourselves forever separated from our true selves." I try to turn him to face me. He pulls away and bends to hoist his victim from the ground.

The others cry in shrill, fervent confirmation.

Lost amid my tribe.

Grendel lifts his prize high above his head. Around me the layered tones of our music resume, louder and stronger than before. Others dance with emboldened hearts, their eyes flashing. Flasks of berry-hued wine pass from one to another with blessings and laughter. The drums—do they set the rhythm of our steps or do our steps set the complexity of their rhythm?—catch and contain one beat within the other, and the sea chamber becomes a collective heart, reverberating with the intoxicating and irresistible buoyancy of our spirit.

We do not know that even then, only a few miles away from our well-hidden, sea-walled world, the destroyer approaches. Our vain glory so fills us with certainty that we do not sense his arrival, the shift in the wind, the lean prow of his boat splitting the sea like a skin with the wound pointed toward us.

With his well-chosen warriors, the Geat named Beowulf sails into the harbor and prepares, even while we sing, to make ground. Beowulf—the only Smallheaded with the strength to match my brother Grendel—arrives with one purpose: to eradicate us from the earth.

As he comes to the shore, we fall deep into a long sleep after our night of revelry. When I awake, the others still doze. Grendel is gone, his robes tossed near his sleeping pallet. I do not see the body of the Scylding warrior anywhere. Yenheth is gone as well.

We are ready to eat our evening meal when they return, anxious and breathless.

"There are new vessels in the harbor, boats longer than the Scyldings' craft. And new and different voices are ringing out from their hall," Yenheth says.

"Perhaps they are here to take the others away," I suggest, my words thin and empty as shells.

Grendel looks at me with scorn. "No, Sister. In this you are wrong. They are not preparing to depart." He turns about and looks at each of us. "Mercenaries have arrived. The Smallheaded Scyldings knew they were about to be vanquished, and their leader's call for help has been answered."

"This explains why my dreams have been filled with more images of battle," Yenheth says. "They may think their call has been answered, but you, my son, shall give them a different answer. You shall vanquish these new warriors and send them all away forever in their grand boats. Grendel, you shall not hunt tonight. Or tomorrow night. Or for several days. The quiet shall unnerve them. They will not know what to do. And then—*then*—you will give them our answer."

Grendel rests. I minister to him and bring him his favorite foods—basted eggs, warm cheese, berries swirled with cream. I massage his arms and legs with rosehip infused oil. He stretches out upon thick cushions near the communal fire and listens to our mother Yenheth. She pulls him to sleep with her words and the rhythm of her incantations and chants; she awakens him with her cries and shouts for glory.

We all believe: He is our savior.

On the night of the next new moon, Yenheth takes Grendel's hand and leads him to the entrance of our sea cave.

As I write, I realize this is the moment at which I no longer think of Yenheth as my mother; I do not even think of Grendel as my brother. I am, simply, just another of the Tribe of Anath. And with the rest of the Anathians, I follow behind Yenheth and Grendel and call out to him praises and blessings. Grendel plunges into the low tide water with a great jubilant roar. We watch as the water ripples, closes over him, and softens back into silence dark as ink.

The others return with Yenheth to the communal fire, humming what has become a war song. They believe our lives soon will be radically different.

I do not join them.

Instead, I follow Grendel.

What possesses me is confusing. I do not relish the idea of observing his brutality, and yet it is magnetic. I do not want to support or assist his efforts, but I am driven by some need to witness his behavior.

Wet and cold, I climb up to the surface and follow at ten reaches behind Grendel, hidden amidst the cover of rocks and their shadows. He moves like an elk over the desolate moorland toward Heorot. Any Anathian normally would have detected me. But Grendel's craving of the death of another Smallheaded has so altered him, he does not sense me even as I feel his heat, the pulse of his neck. Torches burn around the watch path of the hall. As we approach, I see silhouettes of the Smallheaded—both Scyldings and Geats—guarded and braced for the greatest fear.

Smoke from their fires and the growing musk from the thickening sleep of those within the fortress fill my nostrils, and an unfamiliar nausea sweeps over me. Retching, I lean against a tall rock near the entrance to the hall. Unembellished stone pillars, like a dozen sentries facing each other, mark the way to the fortress entrance. Here, Grendel grapples to the top of the outermost pillar and leaps from the top of one to the next, so silent and graceful he moves undetected by the guards posted there.

My brother does not invoke a spell for protection. I think it does not occur to him, and I realize: He has lost all reason. He does not think he needs the ancestors' protection; somewhere between the first murdered Smallheaded and the one he leans toward, Grendel has begun to believe himself immortal.

When Grendel leaps down from the pillar nearest the entrance, the two guards draped in chain mail and bearing heavy standards turn to face him. In the smoky light of the torches above the archway, I see their faces grimace as they shout for others to come to their aid. Grendel is jubilant. I hear his breath rapid with excitement, and know that he, as well as I, feel the foreign and rising heartbeat of the strange warrior they call Beowulf. They call to him, their voices echoing within the interior chamber of Heorot, and Grendel does not pause to consider the threat of the guards. He descends upon the smallest of them, yanks off his helmet, and wrenches his neck. Then he turns and grasps the other guard just as he tries to run into the hall. Grendel does not bother to remove this man's helmet. With two easy twists and one certain snap, Grendel turns him from a struggling, angry warrior into a jangling, dead puppet. He chucks off the warrior's helmet and props the two guards against each other. Using a keen blade taken from his belt, he cuts and splays away their faces until they hang along their chins, their eyes bulging like blown glass bubbles above a collar of bloody skin.

I cling to one of the stone pillars marking the hall's entrance, a vision of what is to come pitches me to my knees. In this vision I see the monster Beowulf lifting my brother's severed arm above his head, blood washing over his face. Grendel's cry of defeat already fills my head. With utter clarity and equal prescience, I realize I hold the power and ability to stop him. I may be younger than he, but when necessary, just as strong, and my magic more refined and schooled than Grendel's. I can make him stop. Can conjure a change in my own shape. Use my magic to drain away Beowulf's strength. Fill the hall with an enchantment of sleep and render all the Smallheaded still and silent. Something. Something else. Something that would move us all toward a different outcome not involving more death.

I want to save something sacred and dear within each of us, and especially within Grendel. But I do not make the leap toward a different outcome. All it would take is a simple turn of thought, in one breath. Something to make the murders end, reverse Beowulf's fate, and pull from his reach the elevation of hero. Turn him into nothing but a visitor. Someone easily forgotten. Someone without a place in myth or legend. Definitely not a future king of the Geats with a name still remembered.

But I do not use my magic. I do not extend my own protection to my brother and do not rush to Grendel's side, pull him away, and shake

26

him from his—what shall I call it at this point? His obsession? His hubris? His madness? Regardless of what would have likely followed—Yenheth's disdain, layers of blame from the others in the tribe, time for the Scyldings and Geats to regroup, find us, and wipe all of us away—I do not try to intercede.

Instead, I press my body into the ground as if it could swallow me whole, and I wait. I listen to my brother as he roars, abandons the bodies of the two guards at the threshold, and plunges deeper into the hall. I cannot move my body or lift my head from the ground to look into the night sky. Clouds clear from the moon and I am washed in moonlight. As if there are no walls to block my view, I watch Grendel enter the mead hall and snatch up the Smallheaded as he comes upon them and tears them apart like bundles of sticks. I watch the warrior Beowulf, gilded in his helmet and armor, bolt across the space between him and Grendel. He lands right before my brother, arms raised and hands clasping his broadsword. With one fluid and dazzling stroke, he strikes at my brother.

They howl at each other like wolves. Their vibrating wails become indistinguishable, and I cannot separate Grendel's from Beowulf's. And from my own throat comes a low and tremulous cry. Our deep keening filling Heorot seems to reach back to an ancient time, drawing together the sorrow of all the generations before us to coalesce here where we are face-to-face with each other. We become a chorus. For one instant, all seems to turn upon the three of us and our lament.

Then Beowulf's handmen charge into the frame of light and sound. The moment shatters like glass. Blades flash. Arms sweep the air. Voices shriek to the challenge of the battle. I witness my vision realized. From the midst of the struggle, Beowulf lifts my brother's arm, the shoulder joint severed clean and bloody. Beowulf roars, bright and glowing. His blade, too, vibrates with light. Images wrap and twist like dozens of birds of prey with wings overlapping and claws gripping. The air fills with sounds of snapping sinew, of bone rending from muscle. Then again, a chorus. Yelps of surprise. Beowulf realizes his victory. Grendel realizes he is not immortal and there is no strong protective magic holding him from his end. His agony.

Grendel turns and his eyes find mine. Granite walls separate us, yet we see each other clearly. Yearning fills his heart. His green eyes, rimmed in gold, sear my own with a deep sadness. He wants my touch. My assurance all will be well. All will be different. As we were long ago in the Labyrinth.

Standing amidst the crazed assortment of his comrades' limbs, torsos, and severed heads, Beowulf stops and stares at Grendel. He lets down his sword and watches Grendel lurch down the main hall toward me, blood pulsing from his shoulder. Beowulf follows him and watches as I enfold my brother into my arms—the way he let me when he was a child and hurt, embarrassed, or both. Grendel presses his face into the curve of my neck, his nose at my ear, his mouth against my jaw. He weeps as he reaches his arm around me.

I whisper the ultimate lie to my brother, "Hush, hush, now love, it will be all right." Children want to believe that. But we are not children. We both know I lie. We both want to believe in my lie.

Beowulf steps toward us. Just one step. He and I look at each other for the first time. Beowulf stands washed in blue moonlight, utterly vulnerable. I can kill him now. Easily. He does not expect it. He will be a victim of surprise and my strength. But I do not move. I hold my brother Grendel and look back at Beowulf. Our hearts beat in unison. I cannot decipher the difference between Beowulf and Grendel's breath.

The web of that long moment does not break until there come the cries of other Smallheaded. I hear the crashing of wooden tables and benches overturned, the wails of women sorting their living from their dead. Someone gives a great howl and rushes up behind Beowulf, breaking the spell and gaining Beowulf's attention.

My brother stands and leans into my arms. Somehow, I gain enough clarity to issue a spell of protection and our images dissolve before the Smallheaded. Grendel and I lunge into the shadows, away.

We stagger across the fen and back to our cavern, drenched in my sweat and Grendel's blood. Before descending to our kin, I turn and look back. Beowulf stands atop the tower at the entrance to Heorot and erects something onto its peak. Too distant to make out clearly, but so familiar that even at a distance, I see it is my brother's arm, displayed upon the tip of Beowulf's spear.

Just as I plunge out of sight with my brother into the salted waves, I hear high-toned glory songs of a war band of the Smallheaded who gather below the tower. My only thought is to take my brother to the safety of our sea cavern.

Grendel should live. The wound inflicted by Beowulf, although severe, is not beyond our healing powers. We summon all our magic and medicine to bring him back to health. Pine rosin covers his left shoulder. Ground amber mixed with myrtle and rue, applied with Yenheth's ministrations and incantations, further knits his flesh together well and strong. Yet Grendel stays curled upon his bed, his moans echoing throughout our dark chambers. We sing to him, plead with him to sit up, take some food, and drink some wine. He only looks at us, his eyes dull as storm clouds, and shakes his head in refusal.

"It is not good," he whispers to me one night when the tide is out and our den fills with hollow longing instead of the sound of washing waves. "They will not stop. There are too few of us. I have failed and we have lost. We have always lost to them."

"No, no, my brother. You must get well. Then we can move on and perhaps find others like us. Somewhere else in the north, or perhaps across the sea, we can make a new home. Far away from the Smallheaded. So far away we will never see any of them again. In the new home we will be stronger and better than here," I say. "We have been a fierce and glittering race since the beginning, just as in our mother's stories. We are still those people. You must believe this, Grendel, you must believe."

He groans, weeping, and rolls over on his sleeping pallet to turn his back to me. His shoulder shakes as he sobs. Then he becomes silent and still. His silence terrifies me. Never have I known Grendel to be so full of despair.

Anguish fills Yenheth as well. She paces around him, reaches out to touch him, to stroke his head, his back. She mews like a wounded animal and when we look at each other, she shakes her head, pulls her hair over her face, and scratches at her chest.

"You must not give up, Grendel," she cries. "That is not our way. You do not go toward death, you make it come to you and make it take you by force."

Yenheth burns sage and sings a song about our ancestors. She lines out the lives of the many members of the Tribe of Anath before us, including Chanan the Labyrinth builder, others skilled in strong magic, those who could render paintings or tapestries in which the subjects moved and lived, those who removed tumors without opening the flesh of the sufferer, those who entered and interpreted dreams with ease and certainty, and those who could impart upon a child the wonder of ciphers and letters. When her voice is hoarse and weary, I take up her song. I do not offer tales of those who passed before us, but poems from our childhood and the things we talk and dream about for our futures. Others gather around us and hum a soft harmony to our songs. And when Yenheth and I can sing no longer, their voices rise in unison into one clear and vibrating raft of sound.

But Grendel is silent.

Grendel is dead.

* * *

Yenheth carries Grendel's body through the arch of the Labyrinth and into the heart of the web of caves. I start to follow her, holding a vial of anise oil and a binding sheet, expecting to join her in the intimate preparation of my brother's body for the funeral pyre.

"Stay here, at the fireside. Leave us be," she cries. Her words send me to my knees, weeping, until one of the elders comes to me, and gently brings me to my feet and guides me to their circle around the smoking flames.

For a long fortnight, her soul-drum mourning reverberates through the shell-curved vaulted sea chambers. We tend the communal fires constantly, grieve for Grendel and await Yenheth's return, when we expect her to share her vision of what we shall do next. The few of us who still gather and hunt during the night witness the Smallheaded around their high funeral pyres, upon which burn the bodies of Grendel's victims. We watch them hoist timbers honed with lancing points as added defensive rims around the settlement walls.

When Yenheth returns to our circle, she collapses into grief. We gather around her, ask when we will commit Grendel's body to the fire and deliver his remains to the sea according to tradition. She bends toward the fire and curtains her head and face with her hair.

"I will not hear of such plans. He is only sleeping. He is still warm. Only in a deep hibernation, as I taught him—as I taught you all—years ago, in case it would ever be needed for a long sea journey. And so he is doing now, to heal his brave soul and restore his valiant heart, and then he will vanquish the Scyldings. He will crush Heorot into rubble and send this tormentor Beowulf away in quaking fear, and the remaining Scyldings with him."

All the others are silent. First one and then another of the elders declare they are too weary. They plead with Yenheth to lead us all away and not think of fighting the Smallheaded any longer. The arguments are thick as the smoke of the communal fire. Yenheth will not be moved. Neither will the elders. They stop arguing with her, turn and leave her alone to rant at the fire.

"So be it. Leave me. Leave and take your pathetic excuses with you. You will regret abandoning your calling. You will be tormented by your cowardice for the remainder of your days." With that, she throws two large cuts of peat into the fire. Sparks fly up and swirl with the smoke, and she walks away without looking at me. Without looking back.

* * *

Yenheth watches over Grendel's corpse and speaks to no one.

The tide rises and falls upon her absence. Those of us who remain of the Tribe of Anath gather in vexation and agree amongst ourselves to flee. With speed and agility, we build a large wood and leather hulled barque, to carry our small grieving band with supplies for a substantial journey, away from this land of dark frustration. We fashion sails from wall tapestries and thick sheeting given to us by the Wanderers—was it so long ago that we were together? As we stack and arrange food supplies and most of our belongings onto the sea craft, I do not want to believe we are going to leave.

We decide to depart during the heart of a moonless night.

Even as we push our craft into the sea, slip through the cavern entrance, and hoist our sails, I hope Yenheth will call out, "Do not abandon me. Return, dearest daughter." Or even more that she will cry out, "Wait. I will come with you. I belong with you, my daughter Rehsotis. We will not be separated."

Just beyond the cove, a wind catches us and pulls us into the sea's arms, soft and steady that night. We sail west over the ink-dark sea toward the unknown and away, we want to believe, from all Smallheaded. I am adrift with my tribe for the span of one moon, my soul as gray and empty as the sea spreading around us. But then vivid images of my mother Yenheth in combat, alone against the many Smallheaded, possess my dreams and even my waking hours. I cannot wrest myself away from the images of her pain, her cries of agony.

I beseech the others to turn around and return for her. They rebuff me with steady gazes dulled by the pain of diminished pride. They pull their hoods over their faces and draw into the quiet insulation of deep sleep, near hibernation.

I make my choice. Buoyed by a wide plank pulled from the largest of the raft-like barques, I plunge into the sea. Cries of remorse and disappointment from the others who have not retreated into themselves press against my back, but I am determined to return to my mother.

I hold myself steady on the wide spine of wood and kick my way back toward land, resting little. Her yearning is strong as a cord pulling me back to her. I have no doubt about where I am going. When I reenter the sea cavern, I am exhausted, but certain I made the right choice. I discover Yenheth sleeping in our den, curled around Grendel's corpse. She has worked strong magic and has coated his limbs with waxy balm made heady with sage and yarrow, and his skin is still smooth and gleaming. I almost expect to see him gasp the fetid cavern air and arise with words of greeting for me.

Silent as a seed I rest next to my mother until she awakens. Without resistance, she lets me take her into my arms and I sing songs of healing and comfort. This gentle time between us does not last, and at evening she pushes away from me. She huddles closer to Grendel and covers her head with her arms. I brew her favorite tea from chamomile and fennel. She pours it into the ground. I braise fish in wild onions and sage. She tastes none of it. Alone with her grief, she does not speak to me. The sea cavern echoes with her wailing grief. I try to touch her, to bring her to me again. But she thrusts away my hands and turns her back to me.

I rest against the archway of the Labyrinth and wish some guidance or comfort would emerge from this remnant of our past. But it is silent, and I wonder if this is my ancestors' way of grieving, of bringing me their heavy sorrow.

In my dreams I rejoin the others from the tribe, and discover them still at sea, and ask them to come back for us. In response, they offer sympathy, but hold to their decision. Their voices grow fragile. They drift farther away. It is more difficult to find them in my dreamscape as well as in the waking dream world.

I stay in the sea cavern. Alone with my mother. And the corpse of my brother Grendel.

One night as the tide returns, when saltwater licks its way again into the entrance of our den, I slip away and swim out into the far reaches of the sea. When at last I surface, darkness surrounds me, and

I float in a star-dusted bowl. No moon. I am lost in a blue-black world. I cannot smell the land. I swim in a circle, sniff the air, search for some land-scent from the shore. But the only smells are of the fervent salt and the passionate mist issued from the sea creatures. I drift until the sun appears in the east and I make my way back to shore.

As I approach the rocky coast, I see a group of the Smallheaded appear at the top of the jutting crags. Some carry smoking torches, others pound skin-covered drums. In pairs, they lug their dead upon slings of canvas down the switchback path to the water's edge. When they reach the pebbled palm of the harbor, they lift their voices in loud cries and wailing shrieks and hoist their dead upon the frame of a waiting pyre. One of the living is dressed in a red cloak, and he throws a burning torch onto the wood and dried seaweed waiting there.

It has been months since Grendel last raged against those in Heorot Hall, and from the scent of these burning bodies, I know these deaths occurred within the last few days. From their yowls, I ascertain they blame my mother.

The group is wrapped by thick vines of smoke and their grief, and they do not notice me as I slip through the water around them and to the opening of the sea cavern. Back in our sea cavern, I find Yenheth kneeling near the communal fire, her hands crusted with dried blood. Her hair falls in tangles over her face. When I come near to her, she does not look up at me. Then I know for certain that Yenheth killed them.

Now every night Yenheth leaves the sea cavern for the surface. And every morning she carries the scent of more blood back into our den.

* * *

Tonight, before she passes into the night, Yenheth draws me into her arms and holds me for a long time, murmuring spells and charms to bring unblemished sleep. She fans my face with an open, scented palm. Then she lightly circles my eyes with the tip of her smallest finger. She chews anise seeds and blows her spicy breath upon my neck and forehead. She massages fragrant black walnut oil against my throat and along my earlobes and hums to me my sleep song. This melody is created for each child by the mother within a few weeks of knowing the child is growing and stretching within the mother's womb; it is the first music known inside our hearts. The somber evening draws over me in a gentle wave and I hold onto her voice as she leaves the cavern:

Kkhor lathar soile.
Kkhor lather soile.
Rehsotis, barhanmei.
Rehsotis, barhanmei.
Kkhon mather ladday.
Kkhon mather ladday.
Rehsotis, barhanmei.
Rehstois, barhanmei.

Heart rest easy.
Heart rest easy.
Rehsotis, music-soul.
Rehsotis, music-soul.
Your mother's heart rests.
Your mother's heart rests.
Rehsotis, music-soul.
Rehsotis, music-soul.

* * *

A few nights later, I return to Heorot Hall and it gleams in gibbous moon-wash. The air hangs heavy with the burnt gristle odor from the line of Yenheth's victims swaddled and stretched along the pathway to the hall's looming door, ready for their final drum-measured journey to the funeral pyre. The cadence of the Smallheaded Scyldings and Geats' songs throbs between the drumbeats, punctuated by the rippling and snapping banners sentried above. Firelight flashes and dances off gold braid-crossed helmets and boar-head shaped shields, glints and sparks off chain mail. Spirits of the dead spiral above the darkening route of their gashed corpses. High and shrill cries for Beowulf penetrate everything.

Then she appears—lurking near enough to the mourning group to reach out and steal one away. Yenheth conjures herself invisible to the Smallheaded, but I see her plain, as do the restless and whimpering pack of hounds gathered and tethered at Heorot's entrance. She wears ceremonial robes dyed larch amber and carries a satchel woven from sweet grass.

My mother. What I remember of her as Mother and not as the Tribe of Anath's leader: the strength of her forearms, the curve of her cheek, the gentleness of her song. Her fervor and energy. In my youth she and I watched the moon together. I pressed my ear against her lavender-scented robe and listened to her heartbeat, a comfort. The carefully ordered hallways of her mind, a reassurance. During those moments we did not construct time. We did not talk. Or at least I choose to remember those nights together in such a way, within the assurance of our shared silence, the measure of time marked upon our breath—when we breathed in unison. How many times did we share such moons? Were there many such nights, or only one—a singular amazing evening alone with my mother, cherished so dearly that my memory now divides and replicates it into hundreds?

She fixes one victim in her mind, and his name is Aeschere, a warrior favored by the Smallheaded's King Hrothgar. She times it well, and even though she has brought night upon night of slaughter, she knows that exhaustion will layer slumber upon even the most terrified of the Geats and Scyldings sheltering in the hall. Yenheth waits until even the guards posted at the hall's gate crumble into sleep at their watch. Yenheth enters undetected, glides among the sleeping Smallheaded, and notices the finer drape of Aeschere's robe and the detailed gold work upon the hilt of his sword resting against the bench at his side. She slips next to the trusted warrior snoring and wrapped in the gift of too much mead, grasps his neck with one hand, clamps the other like a vice upon his chin, and with one furious revolution, rends it from his body as if it were attached only by thin gauze. She tosses his body over her shoulder, lifts his head by his hair like a satchel, and makes her way silently up the granite steps of the hall's tower. At the top she sets down Aeschere's head and body, its blood still flowing, and reaches up to retrieve from the tower's steeple Grendel's arm, its joint crusted by his blood, mingled with Beowulf's. In its place she mounts Aeschere's head—eyes closed and mouth open in a silent howl. With Grendel's arm tucked safe within her cloak, she once again lifts Aeschere's body upon her shoulder and casts it down to the thatch-covered ground below. The guards, less than ten paces away, hear nothing and do not awaken. Like a swift spirit she half climbs, half drifts down the tower's rough surface, picks up Aeschere's body, and carries it to the rock crags nearest the sea. There she finds a protected cranny and buries the body beneath a deep heap of stones and chunks of clay.

When she returns to our cavern, she removes Grendel's arm from her satchel, and with linen thread and many songs of lamentation, stitches it back upon his corpse. In her overwhelming grief, I again become invisible to her. In my frustrated grief, I choose to not reach for her. She makes my brother's corpse whole, and with each stitch, it feels as if we are torn forever asunder.

From cold distance I witness the Smallheaded search for the body of their fallen warrior Aeschere. Beowulf thunders the air around him. He beats his brow into a purpled crown of guilt in not having kept more careful vigil over his comrades. He rallies the Smallheaded toward vengeance—certainly a remaining member of the "vile race" still lurks nearby. With shields and broad swords drawn and ready, they search every cranny and gash in the land around Heorot Hall. When they come to the cliff-edge above our sea-hearted cavern, they cry out in frenzy and believe they see the water steam and burn with Aeschere's blood.

Their soothsayer separates from their ranks and looks down at the sea creatures that loll upon the breakers. He yells and casts rocks at them, as if they are to blame for Aeschere's death. Their teeth and claws dazzle like jewels and with slick ease they dive and rise in the briny depths.

"Just here—I see clearly—the monster resides, a monster who often couples with these tormented beings of the sea," he cries. "Beowulf! Tonight, you shall return here, and you shall find the evil creature who took Aeschere from his rightful place as one of your chosen."

With howls for blood, the Smallheaded crash their shields together and surround their hero Beowulf. He raises his broadsword and leads them in escalating frenzy back to Heorot Hall.

Yenheth sits at her stitching, fashioning large robes from remaining draperies and tapestries. When she finishes, she builds a low and sturdy pyre of dry wood and handfuls of peat and covers this with the robes. She wraps Grendel's body in one of her most beautiful cloaks and binds him into it with braided strips of linen and sage. Slowly she rolls his body upon the pyre and whispers incantations so softly I cannot make out the words. With oil she douses Grendel's shrouded body and from the communal fire lights a torch of switchgrass and seagrass.

Only now does she look at me. The two of us stand, she near Grendel's head and I near his feet, separated by the thickening smoke. She sets the torch-flame against the dry and brittle base of the pyre. The flame catches and with golden sparks and reddening twists, the fire burns higher and the scent of my brother's burning corpse fills my head. "Mother, what has become of us?"

She shakes her head, and then leans back to howl like one of the wild sea creatures hunting just beyond our cavern's entrance. She yowls and advances toward me with her arms raised. I run from her and my brother's funeral pyre—only the echoes of her keening follow me. The sea cave's walls hum and vibrate with her grief, and I seek refuge beneath the arch of the Labyrinth. Its marble certainty lulls my mother's lamentations, and I fall into a fitful, spellbound sleep.

I awaken to find Grendel's pyre a smoldering amber heap. Yenheth stands statuesque at the entrance of the cave, silhouetted dark and equal to the broad-shouldered figure entering the cavern. It is Beowulf, dressed in gilded armor and holding before him a sword nearly half his height. Without hesitation he steps toward my mother.

He does not see me. He is not aware of me, and certainly would not be expecting me. He does not believe there is anyone other than Yenheth here.

"No!" It is a roar. It is a wail. It comes from deep inside of me and turns me into a dark fire. In a rush, I move toward him as he lifts his blade above his head.

"Daughter—"

I am not able to close the gap. He does not even pause, but brings the blade down upon her head. My mother falls to her knees. In flashing reflections against the sea cave walls, the dragon-patterned flat of his sword gleams with her blood. Blood trickles from a gash at her temple. He again lifts his blade, and she pulls from behind her back a steel of her own—one of our own blades, forged ages ago in the valley, used for hunting and long-forgotten ceremonies of sacrifice.

Well placed is her mark when she brings the blade against his helmet, knocking it from his head. She turns and lifts her blade again and strikes his chest. If Beowulf had not been armored, she would easily have split him at his waist. Instead, the blade lodges between two articulated pieces of his armor, and the look of surprise on his face is replaced with a sneer.

His back is within my reach, and I grab at his sword arm just as he again brings his blade down. My grasp is as effective as a moth's wing, and the momentum of his swing is unhindered. The polished sword sings through my mother's neck.

At that moment, I feel her blood run bitter through my own veins. Her pain, her fury, her passion—all coalesce within my own flesh, at the marrow of my bones. My yearning, my desperate need for her love, moves into her body. The force and fire of it all gathers around the blade he holds pressed up against the base of my mother's skull, and in that concentrated moment of my own power, the metal of Beowulf's blade melts like a long taper of beeswax. Beowulf's eyes widen in amazement, and he drops the searing hot handle of his sword and falls back, the tip of the blade, its hilt, and handle clatter to the ground next to Yenheth.

Only then do I hear a cry from her lips. I hear her heartbeat slow and then stop. The cry softens into a whimper and leaves behind a sterling silence. Beowulf stands over the motionless body of Yenheth. He does not move. We stand gasping over my mother's body. The wash of waves fills the cavern. At last Beowulf turns and looks around the chamber. He does not see me. Although I stand before him, close enough to feel his breath, Beowulf does not comprehend that I am there. What strange blindness is this? He turns to my brother's smoldering pyre against the far arching wall of the cavern and makes his way to it with the slow and deliberate step of an arrogant victor. With one foot he topples the balanced mound of delicate ash and bone.

"Leave now or I shall kill you." My words echo loud with sorrow, yet he does not hear me.

He does not flinch.

From the cool ash, Beowulf lifts my mother's blade and leaves.

* * *

In the days following Yenheth's death, I loll in and out of wreck-tortured sleep. I gather driftwood and sea reeds at day, careless of being noticed or seen by the Smallheaded. I coat Yenheth's body with seed oil and crushed heather and sage, then wrap her body in soft reeds, and place her into a cocoon of her yellow cloak — brilliant as autumn sunrise. From driftwood, I fashion a raft. And at the next full moon, I drench her body in more oil and set it alight. Howling, I push my dead mother's body into the night's quiet sea. My cry echoes and is taken up by the sea creatures resting along the shore near me.

The next day I scale the cliff and stagger over the heath toward the fortress of the Smallheaded. Behind the cover of the same tower of rock that kept my presence secret from Grendel so many months before, I watch as the Smallheaded carry large banquet tables out from the hall and cover the surfaces with baskets of brown bread and platters of charred meat. Beowulf emerges in full dress regalia. His companions wear clean and embellished garments.

Hrothgar marches from the entrance of Heorot Hall, robed in fur adorned with wide, gold buckles lined with pearls. He embraces Beowulf again and again.

The Smallheaded drink, eat, sing and dance through the night into morning. When the sun pauses at its highest point, they make way for the harbor, where the Geats' narrow and bowed sea vessels are weighted and waiting. I follow far behind the party of conquerors. Beowulf and his party board their long boats. After more grand speeches and the trumpeting of horns, the warriors lower narrow oars into the sea. They pull their vessels out of the harbor and turn them into the open water. Red sails rise and fill. With the wind to their favor, the ships skim over the sea's surface.

While making my way back to the cavern, I come upon a deer caught in a Smallheaded trap. Her breath is shallow and halting in its panic. Her liquid eyes bulge in alarm. I free her and hold her, stroking her head until she is emptied of life. I use the time to plan what I will do next. I carry her to the entrance of our cavern and retrieve skinning knives and bones and two large baskets. Throughout the night, I gut and skin the doe. In the days that follow, I roast and eat her meat, sucking the marrow from each of her bones. By firelight I work to the rhythm of the waves and pull and stretch her hide over the large baskets to construct my own sea-case.

Ages have passed since I last heard of my own kind using a sea-case. Sometimes, near the end of an Anathian's life, an ill tribe member could elect to leave the tribe enwrapped in this cocoon vessel. If an Anathian woman lost a child and found the grief too great to bear, she might also choose to enter a sea-case. Less often, a tribe member might have a dream in which an ancestor urged a sea-case journey.

Had others of the tribe been near, I would have been the focus of an elaborate feast of rich food, followed by a ceremonious oil-soaked swaddling of my body. Songs of blessings for the journey would have been sung as I would have been stitched into a form-fitting, protective mantle of ecru-colored linen and then carried to a fragrant nest of herbs. The sea-case would have been closed tight around me. I would have been carried into the sea and set to drift away in a deep state of hibernation, not needing food, water, or breath.

Instead, I alone fashion my sea-case to fit around me like a seed pod: strong with a frame of bone and wood. The interior is soft with the deer fur, waterproofed with the oil and rosin from nearby pinion, and beautiful with runes and embellishments I scribe into the pale hide. When the sea-case is ready, I take one final visit to the Labyrinth arch. As I caress the familiar images, a shard of its marble falls to the ground at my feet. I take the lustrous keepsake with me. A token from my tribe.

At the next new moon, I carry my sea-case to the water's edge and stitch myself within it. The tide rolls me into the sound of the sea. I enter a cocoon of sleep so dense, dreams and time cannot find me.

PART TWO

ISLAND

Red light rims the horizon after a fortnight-long gale storm. Brothers Galweth, Patrick, and Aelred heap baskets full of driftwood from the shore when they come upon my large sea-case sphere. They wonder at the leather covering, stiff with sea salt and cold. At last, they contrive a sling of straps and wood to drag me sleeping in my chrysalis to the colossal basket at the foot of the cliff. They heave the sea-case into it and signal to the brothers above, who hoist me up in grating and jagged tugs against the cliff-side

I am pulled from one world and lifted unto another—the Island of the Brothers.

The brothers roll my case-hidden self into the center of their settlement with awe bordering upon fear, pushing me to the communal fire at the foot of a stone cross. The brothers feed pitch-colored slabs of peat to the hungry flames and add dry driftwood until the swelling heat warms the case. It softens around me and my blood stirs.

Brother Angus sits watch. When I move in my cocoon, his heart grows cold as if he expects to feel the icy breath of a demon. He thinks that he should throw me, still swaddled in leather, back into the sea, but even in my hibernation-dulled awakening, I sense a curiosity stronger than his fear. He rubs his eyes and shouts to awaken the fellow brothers dozing a few steps away, just outside a hive-shaped hut's doorway. They cry out and join him at the fire and watch. When my twisting becomes more vigorous, they gasp and cry out. Then Brother Angus slips a dagger between my sea-skin and begins to spread it open. Some expect some unimagined creature to emerge. As the thick hide is peeled away, they realize that what lies beneath is more familiar than foreign.

Edges of fire glow and the silhouettes of the brothers gather and move around me in indistinct numbers. I feel like an abandoned child, long-legged and golden.

The brothers lift and carry me into the warmth of one of their huts. All is muffled and disjointed. I perceive the dance of flames. Brown cloaked shapes move close to me. These hooded figures retreat and leave me in blanketed silence. One offers a constant presence and speaks to me in a rumbling, consoling voice.

I am horrified to find myself amid Smallheaded. I flinch under their touch until I fathom that they do not carry weapons, do not wear any armor. Their thoughts are clear as spring water and entirely made up of questions—not judgment, murder, or destruction. Within the thickening murmurs of their protection, I begin to feel an alien but glistening sense of safety.

The brothers cover me in one of their long brown gowns and they wrap my feet and legs in soft skins. The brother with the comforting voice manages to comb through my hair and plaits it with careful, compassionate fingers. I see that we move with a similar quiet and reserve, and draw comfort from that, although I stand a full head taller than any of them and am leaner and move with greater fluidity.

They speak in soft tones, and their words are not as harsh as the words of the other Smallheaded. An order and a finer melody resides in their language; they speak with words built upon a musicality. At regular intervals throughout the day, the brothers gather and proceed to a common hall, which they call *chapel*, and here their words thrum and roll over their tongues in thick full-barrel tones. Their words line out into the sunlight, a long, steady trail. The language approximates my own Anathian tongue, and in little time I understand even the subtleties.

The small Island of the Brothers becomes a companion. It is an impossible place, better described as a ledge of rock, a surging of rock out of the sea. There are only two ways to reach the settlement of the brothers—by being pulled up in the basket or making a precarious ascent up five hundred stone steps, each quarried and set into place by the brothers.

The gentle-voiced Brother Angus tells me, "It took ten of us to put a section of rock in place, each blessed by prayers and sweat."

The steps lead to a narrow saddle between two stone columns over which are inscribed with intricate patterns and images of long-toothed lions and multi-headed birds of prey. Brother Angus tells me they are described in the book of their god. A large cross crowns each column. One is carved with prayers for the dawn and the other with prayers for the night. After passing between the columns, I follow the stone path to a high vista where I survey a gentle sloping bowl in the thin-skinned earth. There, a walled monastery stands, built from the same glinting rock as the steps. Just outside the gate stand twelve hive-shaped stone huts arranged in a long crescent; here reside contemplative pilgrims, some of whom chose to make amazing promises and take extraordinary vows, by which they gain entrance and residence in the monastery proper.

At the north side of the monastery rises the tallest peak on the island—a rocky, hulking tower of white stone marbled with moss and lichen. At its summit stands yet another cross, this one the most elaborate, made from all the gold brought to the island by brothers alive and dead, and pilgrims by the hundreds. The cross stands before what the brothers call the kneeling stone. Unique and startling in its blood-red color, the stone, the brothers believe, is not from this part of the world, but has been set down upon that spot by the actual hand of their god. The kneeling stone garners powerful significance. The brothers regularly make their way, alone or in groups, to the stone and the cross; there they kneel, embrace the engraved stone symbol of their faith, and ask to be burdened with all that their god asks of them. This involves a great deal of loud prayer and even more silent tears. At first it amuses me, and I await some breach in their intense sincerity. But after many months, I grow to not only tolerate, but appreciate it. At moments, their music reminds me of the music we made as a tribe.

Within such peacefulness, I dwell with the brothers. They call me God's Orphan.

* * *

Quiet conversations with Brother Angus fill my days following my arrival at the monastery. The contemplative rhythm of time within the sanctity of my small hive-dwelling is also marked by unvarying visits from Brother Galweth and Brother Patrick bringing food and drink. As time passes, their general greetings and queries about my health begin to include other questions about from whence I came and whether someone might be searching for me

I ask them some of the same questions, and Brother Angus tells me he is the leader of this new settlement of believers of, as he called it, Our Lord God. He tells me he heard of other creatures like me, living in the northernmost reaches of the great sea, but they are legends from long ago. I tell him a little about the Tribe of Anath and our journey north. But I do not tell him much more. When I braid his stories and recounting of legends together with the timing of Grendel and Yenheth's murders, I determine that at least sixty winters passed from the time I left the sea cavern until I washed upon the shore of the Island of the Brothers.

The rhythm of my days soon follows the pattern of the brothers' lives, and I assume duties shared among them. Before dawn I awaken and help prepare the midday meal—a porridge of mashed grain mixed with crumbled remains of the previous day's barley loaves, soaked in fermented grain water. The brothers gather around the stone and timber cross looming at the center of their settlement, offer morning prayers, and then go to their tasks. We tend traps tucked into the small shrub groves dotting the island and check nets set in leeward coves. At midday all gather at the central low-roofed hall with walls of stone and assume their places on the benches in the large gathering room encircling a smoking fire. Each brother holds a plate and cup; upon each plate I portion their gruel, into each cup I pour the dark beer. After a time, some of the brothers will ask how I am, will compliment the mix of the gruel, or sigh in gratitude for the beer. Most of them do not acknowledge me, and after several months, even those who at first trembled when I came near no longer seem to notice. After I serve them, I slip into my seat at the back and listen to Brother Angus read from the large book he removes with proud care from a locked chest fitted with metal.

For evening meals, we add flakes of fish or morsels of small game and wash it down with beer carried in pitchers from the domed hut dedicated to several casks of fermentations. Sometimes this plain diet is varied with the cured and salted meats that arrive as gifts for the brothers in pilgrims' baskets.

* * *

During spring on the Island of the Brothers, we work in the gardens scratched into the thin skin of soil and grow purslane, fava beans, caraway, anise, and fennel. The sea currents change, and during our daily visits down to the shore we find a greater variety of fish and increased heaps of driftwood for our fires. We fill baskets with scavenged berries and seeds.

When not gathering food or fuel, the brothers engage in their finest work. At one end of the hall where meals are taken sit two long rows of tables, each supplied with clay lamps, rough-hewn benches, sets of jars filled with ink, and boxes filled with nibs and brushes. Along the walls are books and scrolls organized upon shelves or in stacks of chests. Here beats the collective heart of the settlement. With the most senior and devoted checking their work, a select number of brothers transcribe and illuminate page after page of their holy book. At first light, they sink into their work, enthralled by the contents of the lines of script upon which they are carried until the evening ration of lamp oil burns out.

I learn during the early years with the brothers that by keeping my reserve, I am not only tolerated, but nearly forgotten. I watch and listen. Threads of conversations overheard in the garden spin into a raiment of understanding. Arguments in the gathering places continue even as I approach. I learn Brother Aelred is too protective and miserly with his distribution of the thin sheets of gold leaf to even the most artistic and skilled of the brothers. Songs the younger brothers sing to themselves often have nothing to do with holy pursuits. They live in fear of the recurring fever, which drives many families to send their sons to the monastery. New arrivals recite their language lessons within my hearing, and their constant practice becomes my own.

I overhear Brother Angus speak about me with some of the brothers in the hall of scribes. "I am glad to have her assuming most of the cooking and washing chores. She takes good care with these duties. Because of her ceaseless stamina our charges need not spend as much time on physical preparations. They can pursue Our Lord God's truth for even more portions of their day. She is indeed, as you say Brother Galweth, a gift from Our Lord God."

"I find her appearance distressing." Brother Aelred strokes and turns the sheets of vellum spread before him.

"Despite her appearance, she is a gentle soul." Brother Galweth hands a finished illuminated page to Brother Angus for approval.

"She is a child of Our Lord God, Brother Aelred." Brother Patrick sets down a pot of ink loudly enough to make the others flinch and look toward him. "And her soul, I do believe, is pure."

"I agree she is a child of Our Lord God, but I am less convinced of the quality of her soul, Brother Galweth and Brother Patrick. Now return to your duties. Keep vigilant to her habits."

Brother Angus leaves the hall with a confirmative nod to Brother

Aelred.

* * *

Amid the company of the brothers, the weight of my loneliness becomes unbearable. Daydreams fill with scenarios of one of the Tribe of Anath living on a nearby island. Night dreams groan with longings that someone of the tribe seeks me. Each night I unlock my dreamscape and seek the solace of the chambers of a kindred heart. But every night is a dark and empty bell, with my hope like an echo against the dream walls of others who are not of my tribe.

But by engaging in a dream quest with such dedicated frequency, one night I enter the vulnerable dream space of Brother Angus. I find him fighting against the force of a strong storm at sea. He sails alone in a small boat at first. Then the water disappears and he is stranded in the middle of a vast desert. Naked and lost, he walks across the desert, the sand opens beneath his feet, and he falls into a dark pit, surrounded by familiar faces contorted with hideous grimaces. Then all the faces transform into faces like mine. Brother Angus turns and runs toward a line of Smallheaded draped in glorious cloaks, clasping golden crosses and icons of their faith. He grasps his own crucifix and presses his body close to it. He rises upon it like a falcon and flies it into the dark, above sand and desert, to a landscape where all is green and marked by giant rocks and splintered boulders. Then Brother Angus, upon the wings of this cross, turns and sees me in his dream. A dark wall of alarm begins to rise from him and, although I try hide myself, his alarm shuts me out of his dream.

That next morning, Brother Angus awaits me in the gathering hall when I enter to begin making the daily rations.

"Did you sleep well, Orphan?"

"Very well, Brother Angus. Your concern is a blessing to me."

"I had a troublesome dream." He sits on a stool next to me at the table where I cut barley crusts. He retells the dream and watches my every move. "And what would you make of such a dream?"

I look into his eyes and find the reflection of the flickering fire reduced and trapped there. He does not flinch. I do not sense fear from him, but a clear curiosity.

"You know dreams, don't you, Orphan?"

The silence is interrupted by a log falling in the firepit. Brother Angus will need to leave soon to lead the brothers in prayer. His earnest request makes me brave.

"I do know dreams, yes. All of my tribe know and believe in dreams." I turn and add the barley crumbs to the porridge pot.

"With such knowledge, what value do you place on the one I just told you?"

"You already know it has value." I brush the barley crumbs from my hands and stir the thick, fragrant grains with such vigor my wooden paddle clatters against the side of the iron pot. "You struggle to find a place to fulfill your dreams. You are wary and vigilant about threats to those dreams. You face many hard choices, and you must keep a relentless grip on what you believe in order to transcend these fears."

This is a lie. It is what he wants to hear. And what he wants to hear will keep me safe. I know this as certain as the salt I stir into the steaming pot. His pleasure in my interpretation brings a gentle curve of satisfaction to his mouth.

"Yes. Your words are well-spoken." He quietly leaves and I soon hear the call and response of the morning prayers.

Brother Angus and I talk often about his dreams. Sometimes he even asks about mine. We discover his religion's tradition of interpreting dreams is similar to my own tribe's. I embrace this offered thread of authenticity and it relieves me to be seen, to have a part of my nature, if not valued, at least noticed and acknowledged.

One evening Brother Angus, Brother Galweth, and Brother Patrick come to the storage hut where beer and mead are kept and find me stirring the crocks filled with yeasty brew. They are warm and gregarious after a full supper and several large goblets of the thick beer, and Brother Angus asks, "And what of your dreams these nights, Orphan?"

"These nights of late I am so weary, I deem the pain of my limbs and hands prevents me from the ability to grasp any fiber of story or meaning from my dreams."

"Understood. These days are full, and our burdens intense. The garden harvest waits for no one." Brother Galweth offers a sympathetic sigh. "We cannot hurry too much to bring in the garden's yield."

"Perhaps that is why all I have dreamt of late involves turnips and squash." Brother Patrick peers at us from beneath a grizzled brow with twinkling eyes.

Our laughter marks an opening through which word of my dream-reading spreads throughout the brotherhood.

"The Orphan is gifted in understanding dreams," says one to another. Daily, a brother seeks me out, looks around as if afraid to be caught in some illicit act, and asks for my interpretation of the images carried from the night into day. Then, when it seems everyone is comfortable in the commonality of this knowledge, the brothers approach me warmly and often—in the garden amid heart-leafed bean vines and brushy fennel stems, along the beach picking out the largest lengths of driftwood, or in quiet stony corners after evening prayers.

"Please, Orphan," a brother begins, "here is my dream. Divine its meaning for me."

* * *

Most of the brothers are young men, sent by their parents to a place perceived as safe, where comforts, such as food, clothing, and knowledge, are easily gotten. Some families believe that by sending their sons to the brothers, they ensure the entrance into after-death paradise for the entire family—souls, brokered to the brotherhood. Others even hope their sons will become the next leader of the brotherhood, driven by visions and faith.

But despite their families' spiritual aspirations, the young men are driven by longings of the flesh. They all want their dreams to be full of significance, something holy to elevate them above the others. Yet the images of which they tell me are sensual details of the thighs of the young women they love, the curve of a young woman's neck, or the scent of blooming plum trees arching above their spring passions. Certainly, some seem to think I will one day be amazed by a dream, share it with Brother Angus as nothing short of a miraculous vision, after which the dreamer will be placed at the supper table to the right hand of Brother Angus—as their prefect Elijah reborn, here to establish his own outpost among all the unclean and unclaimed heathens of these islands and north shores.

But nothing like this happens. None of their dreams interest me enough to have me enter their dreamscape myself.

None but Brother Angus's.

My dreams and his continue to entangle in moonlit webs. Each night I am drawn into his dreamscape filled with opaque images of faces so much like my own, images that linger through my day. It is as if Brother Angus knew of me and my kind before my arrival upon their island shore. After evenings when he drinks excessive quantities of beer, he sleeps without any mental guard, and his dream gate opens with ease, and I push my dream-self into the realm of his night. After strings of nights, dancing in the midst of faces like mine, I encounter the image of the being who is like me, but is strong-jawed and clear-eyed. His distinction attracts me. I return to him again and again, and I began to think of him as my Other.

One night in deep winter I do not pull through layers of drape-thick images in Brother Angus's dreams to reach my Other. In this dream, Brother Angus sits in the scriptorium, under the red flame of the lamp the brothers keep burning there. He is waiting, but not for me. I cloak my dream-presence in the dark recesses of his mind and linger with equaled expectancy. And then my Other appears.

My heart drums in my chest in a mixed rhythm of fear and excitement as I realize this is not a mere dreamscape image or shadow. This is a detailed recollection of an encounter with someone who exists in the realm of reality, and not just in the essence of a story. Here is another Anathian—in Brother Angus' dream.

Brother Angus turns to my Other and just as they are about to embrace, my Other sees me. He looks at me over Brother Angus' shoulder and his eyes narrow as if to see me in better focus. The two of us are aware of each other's presence in Brother Angus' dreamscape. Brother Angus does not understand what is happening at first. I emerge from the shadows of his dreaming mind. My Other steps away from Brother Angus and moves to me, reaches out, and touches my cheek. He and I are in the midst of more than a dream, floating through the dreamscape of a Smallheaded. I feel the heartbeat of my Other. It is strong and real, and not muffled as is common within dream encounters. My Other and I meet in Brother Angus's dream with images so clear, we know this is present tense. Both of us are alive. Immediate.

Brother Angus trembles and thrashes about in his sleep. He works to reclaim his own space in his dream. My Other and I slip away and apart from each other in a glimmer. I am beside myself with joy. In the heat of the nightscape in my hut, I cast about for the heat of my Other, seek his lingering image in the mist of Brother Angus' dream, but it is lost. Brother Angus' fear and trepidation dissipates our own ability to find each other—the traces of each other's presence lost.

With the clear-edged dawn, I recognize that I am not alone. Brother Angus knows another like me.

And even more, my Other lives near and at hand.

* * *

The Dream of the Spiral points to always, and turns around the Point of Origin. That is the heart of the Labyrinth, and it pulses deep into my dreams. Each night my dreams of my Other grow stronger. I dwell in the Other's rhythm, and my thoughts keep pace with his. From the depth and textures encompassed in his dreams, I determine he is an elder and he rests not far from the monastery on the Island of the Brothers. Winter sea storms are strong enough to bring towering waves of force to the craggy cliff edges of the settlement. We huddle in the dining hall to hoard our heat. The storms rage upon us, and we are close to gray despair when the sun tears open a seam in the angry heaven to reveal a raiment blue as heron wing. With upturned faces we gather around the central cross and bask in the golden sun's warmth. Brother Angus calls for a grand communion, and this ritual fascinates me. The brothers believe a fervent partaking of the body of their Lord signifies their redemption. The celebrants finish the drone of weaving words and launch into songs of praise.

The songs drift into tuneful melodies, and Brother Angus shakes his head. "You sing simple-minded mead-hall songs changed to suit my holy expectations."

He does not stop them, but leaves them to their warbling while he and a handful of elder brothers assemble in the library, where their more serious deliberations transpire in relative peace.

I walk away from the lingering group of brothers and past the hall, drawn to the edge of the rock ledge by the drift and shift of a shape that is not waving grass or feathering heather. Just a mere wisp of a cloak. My Other is there, and I resist the impulse to run to the crest of the knoll and find him. Instead, I carry mead and honey cakes to Brother Angus and his circle in the library and then take calm and collected leave of them before returning to my hut.

Well into the night, when I am certain the brothers slumber deep beneath the lingering comfort of their night full of song, food, and beer, I pack a satchel of bread and dried seeds. In the brief sighting of my kindred spirit, I sensed pain. So I also pack a kit of healing tools and remedies—pierced bones to use as needles and softened reed fibers, sage oil, roasted moss, and small rolled balls of propolis.

The full moon floods my doorway with tremulous light. I breathe in the glowing air, close my eyes and listen to all the beating hearts around me. It is easy to sort through them all and find the one I want. The heart echo of my Other is stronger than all the others. I know he is awake. With strong and silent strides, I take the north path from the monastery that runs parallel to the island's shore. The surf pounds a wrenching rhythm far below me. Waves scatter moonlight and phosphorescent beads of sea life into a glowing foam. Each rush of waves says, "He is there. He is there." I break into a run that matches the rushing voice and it grows louder. The heartbeat of my Other drums a fearless urging. *"Here. Here. Here."*

I reach the land's end and fall to my knees. A ragged narrow ledge of rock edges back and across the cliff face below me. The moon's light illuminates rock steps descending into a hollow of darkness. Perhaps the opening into a cave. With my satchel secured around my waist, I begin my descent. The sea surges beneath me when I reach the rock shelf at the water's edge. Saltwater washes over my feet, and I crouch to regain my balance against a rogue wave. The cave's mouth is twice my height and only as wide as my shoulders. I enter the chamber and the heart echo of my Other pounds against my own chest.

He sits with his back to me, close to the amber flames of a well-built fire, wrapped in a golden cloak woven through and embroidered with richly detailed figures and images from Anathian legend and history. It is the cloak of a tribal elder and language keeper. I stand silent in tears and watch him.

When he turns to look at me, his mouth is curved in a gentle smile and his eyes are as dark as the night. He spreads his cloak around him in one liquid motion and with an open hand, invites me to sit next to him. I say nothing, kneel next to him, and push my satchel full of food and herbs toward him. He lifts the satchel with ease and opens it. He smiles and my heart turns into a dove.

"I am Rehsotis."

"Yes, I know. I am Yargis."

He opens the satchel while still studying my face, then turns his attention to the contents as if they are gifts.

"These are good things." He inhales the cardamom fragrance of the barley loaf and tears it into two equal halves. He hands one to me. "I can add to this."

He releases the clasp of his cloak and it drifts down from vaulted shoulders. When he stands, the glint of something metal sways from his hip. With gliding step, he crosses to a dark corner of the cave and returns with two alabaster cups brimming with a clove-fragrant wine. After handing one to me, he kneels to face me and takes up his bread, and lifts the cup and crust to me as if in formal blessing. We eat the bread, drink the wine, and only then begin to talk.

* * *

To know such intimacy: the glint of eye, the warmth of voice. A heart companion. Such bliss and joy. The time Yargis and I share is sacred and priceless. Even when with him, I long for him—for the next appreciative story, look, touch. I dwell within his voice for several days. We sleep little. Meals are simple banquets of fish, bread, herbs, and wine. Most of all, we talk.

For seemingly countless afternoons we rest upon an outcropping of rock near his cave, the sun easing our joints. My back feels as if warm liquid flows over it. The calm seas swirl with sunlight just below our feet.

We languish beneath a sky so blue it seems as if we belong in a different land, one where there are no Smallheaded. Yargis reaches a hand to mine, his touch skilled and tender. I bask in his voice, relish his form, savor the rich scent of his skin. My eyes close. My hands caress his arms up to his shoulders, then neck, and down over the wide smooth spread of his chest. He does not move away, but leans into my touch. I feel an intake of breath beneath my hand and he rolls, turning closer to me.

"You are so innocent." If his lips were not at my ear, I would not have been able to hear these soft words. "Do you understand what your touch invites? What you offer? What I feel?"

I open my eyes and look into his, our faces so close we exchange breath. "I know that my dreams are filled with you. We are among the last, if not the last, of the tribe. But even if there were many others, if we were two among hundreds, I would still seek you out. I am not innocent of desire."

"What, my dear Rehsotis, what do you want?" His voice breaks. The heat of the sun, the warm rock, my own blood, all thicken within a moment. In answer I stretch my body along the length of his and rest my head against his shoulder.

"Then it shall be as intended. The sea is ready."

He guides my legs to wrap around his hips and with his arms around me, we slip into the water. The water's fierce cold takes away my breath and we turn together into the waves, falling deeper into the cove. His mouth covers mine and I am spread open, arms outstretched like wings, back arching, and Yargis enfolds me into his warmth. We drift deep into the water, spiral and grasp each other in a watery dance. Now I am not cold. Not frightened. We do not need to breathe. We do not breathe. Instead, the water fills us with more desire for each other. We turn around each other. I mimic his every gesture and touch, over the arm, across the back, from foot to groin, neck, ear, lips—with each touch we dismantle all sense or dimension of self. He repeats each gesture and caress I offer his body. I cannot determine where his skin is in relation to my own. Saltwater mixes us together. We turn into something else, another version of ourselves as liquid as the sea yet solid as marble. We roil around each other, my tongue hot between teeth, lips, fingers. His back like ribbon. My legs like banners. And there are the colors—colors that fill our minds. Red deepens to violet; yellow plumes open into emerald. A pounding begins at the small of my back—my passion wants more darkness—and pure light issues from our mouths.

I wonder if we are rocked by the motion of the sea and its deep current so far below the surface or if we cause a new tide. It is both. It does not matter. We grasp and clutch and suck and lick and taste and stroke each other. All heat. All salt. Water mingles with breath. The two of us double upon each other again and again and again. We become part of the sea; we push against the rocks and fall farther into the deep. It is dark and destructive, dangerous and completely understood. Utter desire. Time does not account for us, and we give it no notice. It seems to take only a moment and yet we turn into a liquid forever. Everything expands and contracts at the same time. I want never to surface, but to descend farther, press always so close to Yargis.

And then the gentling of the movement. A gaining awareness: Here is his hand, these are his eyes, this is my arm. We begin to reconstruct each other and, as we do, we surface, ascend to the light above. We are two again, our bodies lift, our heads break into the air. We are spent, and float at rest, one with the other. Then with long, slow strokes, we regain the shore.

* * *

Memories of the tribe fill my mind—my mother stroking my hair as she told a story, my brother Grendel laughing in a game of chase, the elders around the communal fire, the sunlight turning the Labyrinth dust into golden answers. Other recollections press from memory into present tense upon waves of painful encounters. Our passion ushers them into my mind. A shell named denial is cracked, and all vulnerabilities are released. My salty dreams of origins turn into regular breaths, coalesce into words, and I speak them. The stories of my past issue like unstrung jewels upon Yargis, and he nods in a deep understanding ripe as the plums and ground cherries we feed each other.

My breath is his. Every other thought, if not every thought, echoes against the name *Yargis, Yargis, Yargis*. The sound of the sea contains each syllable. His beauty. My beauty. And through our sensual enjoyment of each other, I revel again in a joy for living.

I do not want to leave his side. We return to the rock shelf and the mouth of the cave, and I curl within his embrace. He wraps us like a cocoon in his red cloak, and he tells me again the stories woven therein.

Yargis tells tales of his truth, and sometimes he offers poems.

Most often stories. The liquid roll of his voice offers me singular images, names, and narratives, and then he slips them like pearls onto the string of my imagination. He retells Anathian legends I remember from long ago fire-banked evenings when the tribe was blessed. I fall into a dream-mead enchantment. After an evening of storytelling, we return to the sea for moon-engorged passion.

Then we wash each other in fresh spring water, stroke each other with lavender-infused oil, and ease each other into warm robes. And again, I am eager to listen to whatever Yargis cares to tell me.

One story centers upon the life of Rexnalli, the keeper of fire, and Cadlum, the winter maiden.

"No two lovers were ever more consumed by each other."

"Until now." My soft laugh is dark as amethyst.

He touches my lips with a gentle finger and continues. "But you see, even though Rexnalli's gift of fire was a blessing for our kind, it was a curse for Cadlum. She craved and sought his burning touch, but too much of it—and she would turn to water. And if Cadlum were to turn to water, she jeopardized her lover Rexnalli's life. Yet, they could not bear to be parted for long and certainly not forever. Finally, their passion for each other overcame fear for their own lives. But because they were so in love, their passion simply turned one into the other— fire into ice, ice into fire. So they tasted of each other and spent tender, truncated time within each other's world, and were careful to part from each other just at the moment of no return—before it would be too late to return to their true nature and all would be ruined.

"But if they kept turning from one form into the other, didn't they keep missing each other?

Yargis looks at me and sighs. "The children of my tribe never asked such questions."

"I am not a child."

He smiles, and from the tenderness of the kiss that follows the smile, I realize how well he understands how far from childhood I have traveled.

We tease and caress each other around and between our exchange of legends and tales. In exchange for a story, I dance or sing for him. For one of mine, he takes up a round-backed lute, not as beautiful as those I crafted, but possessing a clear and winsome tone. We take turns playing comfortable lullabies or strumming winsome improvisations.

I treasure stories about his life the most. For hours, I listen to him talk about his ancestors who were the first to leave the Valley of Origin, despite protests from the others of the Tribe of Anath. They found another fertile valley farther north and built new homes. There were several small settlements of Smallheaded nearby, but the recurring fever arrived and took all of their lives. Anathian are immune to the Dark Plague, so after the pestilence scrubbed away even the ghosts of the Smallheaded, Yargis and his tribe lived and thrived there for hundreds of years until another a band of Smallheaded arrived, settled, and this time endured. The recurring fever did not return, the Smallheaded increased in number, and so did tensions between them and his tribe. Again, the band of Anathian to whom Yargis belonged decided to leave and seek another place in which to dwell in peace.

One story breaks my heart.

"I need to tell you why I left the tribe and came to live alone." Yargis draws me close into his arms, weaves his fingers into my hair, and kisses my forehead, eyelids, mouth.

"I am glad you left the others. If not, we would not have found each other here."

His lips move across my breasts, over my hips and thighs. The heat of our lovemaking liquefies the air of the cave. We tangle ourselves within the pallet robes for long velvet hours before either of us speak with words again. I nudge Yargis and urge him to finish the story.

"These centuries have been lonely."

"But not now. You are here now." With his whisper the fire mellows into the deepest amber.

Another kiss.

I know my heart is about to be torn apart. But as it does, he gathers together the fragile pieces with his tenderness.

"I once loved a woman named Karsana. She was the daughter of my tribe's matriarch, promised to become the wife of a tribal elder who was a healer, and much loved by the tribe. I did not intend to fall in love with Karsana, but we would find ourselves standing next to each other at evening songs. We would laugh at the same time during evening banquet. When I told tribal stories my gaze would be drawn to her luminous face. I would speak to her eyes, and the warmth from those eyes seemed to envelope me like a warm spring sigh. We would find increasing reasons to meet each other at the well, or the common fire, or the gardens. We did not need to speak of when or where."

My heart clenches with the tightening rhythm of jealousy. I cannot look into his eyes.

"Do you want me to go on?"

I listen to the waves, the rustling embers that fall in the silence after his question. "Yes. I do. I know it was long ago and not possible, but there is a huge part of me who wishes it could have been me. I am jealous of someone in your past. That is not rational, but you are telling me about her, so she is important."

Yargis adjusts the robes around our shoulders and pulls me closer. "Finally, I could not bear to stay. She was not to be mine, and I could not live near her if she could not be. I left the tribe without a word, without explanation. None was needed. But Karsana followed. She found me in the mountains, miles from where my tribe had settled. I told her she needed to return. That she needed to honor her marriage agreement. When she could see that I would not be moved, she kissed me, turned, and ran away down the mountain path toward the ledge. I watched in disbelief as she flung herself into the night, outlined for just a brief moment against the full moon. And then she fell. She was gone. She may have taken the leap herself, but it was as if I had thrown her to her death. I ran to the ledge and looked down, saw her silent form so far below. Such a silence. And then I left. I moved on. I was a coward. An unforgivable act."

"But you were both young," I whisper. "We all do things we later regret." I think of how I did not act to stop Grendel. How I did not do more to claim my voice with my mother. My own deeds.

He shakes his head. "Perhaps. Perhaps. But you need to know this about me.

At that, I wrap my arms around him and offer all comfort to him "I felt jealous of Karsana. But now, I feel a warm affection for her. An understanding for you both. She could not go on. You did not know she would do such a thing."

"I should have stopped her. Or I should have let her come with."

"But you did not. You both did what you thought you had to do." I do not tell him my bittersweet realization that if he had stopped her or if he had let her come with him, I would not be with him now. I cannot imagine life without him. I do not want him to be in pain of memory, but I believe my love for him will ease that regrettable act and that the same realization might stir in him.

* * *

I awake to find myself alone in the chamber. I turn to the sun- filled entrance and see Yargis sitting at the ledge. I wrap myself in a soft robe and go to him. In silence he draws me down into his arms and we sit together as the sun climbs from a red cradle into a high bowl of golden heat. He takes my hand and places in my palm a small egg-shaped piece of glass on a thin braid of leather and gold-link.

"This is a burning glass. Let the sun flow through it like this, and you will always be able to start a fire. You do not even need that much light. I have been able to use moonlight, and it will create a flame."

He shows me how to turn the thicker end around in my palm until it catches and streams a thin finger of golden light upon a dry piece of reed he rests crumbled between us. The reed smokes and then flares into a brief blaze.

"It can also be used to burn out wounds in the same way, or to melt wax or sap into a seam on the hull of a watercraft. I have even roasted apples with the light it can collect." He sits up taller as if straightened by pride for the stone.

"Many uses for something so beautiful." It feels warm in my hand. "I want you to have it. Keep it with you always. You have brought light and warmth into my life. Now you can carry some of that from me with you—always."

He opens the chord's clasp and fixes it around my neck. It rests heavy and splendid between my breasts.

The brothers wonder where I am. They miss their dinner, then breakfast, then dinner, again and again—a long string of missed meals. Even though I sense their growing frustration, I do not leave Yargis. I do not return to the monastery for several moons, but spend them all with Yargis—my lover, my Other, my missing self. And while we are together a dead calm settles over the sea—even the sea spreads itself smooth as a sleeping pallet and welcomes our repeated descents into it during the star-swept nights. When we wrap around each other in the sea, we are without age, without limits. His age dissolves. He is a wild young lover equal to my desires, my passions. Each question made by the touch of my hand, the press of my lips, is answered by his own.

* * *

I decide to tell Brother Angus and the others about Yargis.

At first Yargis discourages me and suggests that we simply steal away and make our way to a secluded island. "Somewhere south of here, and warmer, where my old joints will remain supple enough for your enthusiasms."

He almost persuades me.

"I want them to know. Despite everything, they offered sanctuary. I expect understanding." And with those words, I make my way up the ledges and rocky steps of the skellig. When I walk through the monastery entrance and back down between the rows of hive-shaped cells, I am greeted with stony stillness. Even the common fire is banked and smoldering.

Brother Angus stands at the doorway of his cell and watches me approach. I come before him; he turns and I follow him inside.

"Where have you been?" His voice matches the fire-charged shadows of the cell's interior.

"Following my own dreams." I stand just inside the doorway. "Your dreams. What do you mean by that?" He is shaking.

"I have found another like me, Brother Angus." I keep my voice low and steady.

As I tell him about finding Yargis, Brother Angus bows his head and turns to face the fire, his back to me. When I finish speaking, we stand looking at each other, and I can hear our rapid heartbeats.

"What you are about can come to no good. You must know that." Each word is a beat, heavy as a stone falling onto dry earth. "What you are doing is not acceptable to God."

"What do you mean? How can you say such a thing? You know how alone I have been." I come to stand closer to him, my hands lifted in supplication.

"It is because of what I witnessed. One night, out of concern for you and where you went, I wandered to the far end of the island. At the rock's edge, thinking you may have fallen there, wondering if you were hurt or dead, I looked down into the sea and… and I saw you there with this Other you describe. I watched as the two of you fell into the sea. I witnessed an act not acceptable to God. An act of monstrous vulgarity," he hisses.

"Your act even affected the sea. The water in the cove at first grew calm and then rolled into a steady roil until a red vapor rose from the waves. The vapor became a thick cloud that lifted and thickened until it swathed the moon in a blood-streaked haze. Even some of the brothers awoke in the night, and in searching for the moon, found it cloaked by the red scrim." Brother Angus shakes his head in decided disapproval. "They were frightened by what they saw that night. The next morning, I heard them talking before breaking their fast. They said, 'Did you see the moon in its crimson mantle? It must be a sign. A portent. Brother Angus must ask the Orphan, certainly she will know.' On and on they whispered, and when they found you still absent, you can imagine the rumors, the terrible stories they formed and sent spiraling through our numbers."

The images of which he speaks are reflected in his eyes—the other brothers, especially some of the younger ones, full of wonder as they watch the sky while Yargis and I coupled in our mutual hunger.

"Then they all gathered around me," Brother Angus continues. "All of them certain something terrible was about to happen. Many of them believe that your disappearance and the altering of the moon to be bad omens. And so I told them. I told them it was not a sign of goodness. I told them something wicked is at the source. Something of the old ways, the ways we are trying to eliminate. I told them God does not arrive in red clouds. I told them to pray with their greatest devotion to have this anathema removed from our firmament."

As he speaks, I see some of the other brothers shuffle near the doorway. Brother Angus' words hang heavy upon their hearts, and they bow their heads in disappointment and fear. How will I bear this? Again, the Smallheaded are filled with fear of the Anathian, and it is because of me.

"Often I have looked into your cell in these past months, hoping to find you returned to us. The others did so as well. But your pallet was empty. Your table, clean and orderly. And now you return. What are you about?" Brother Angus lifts his chin and glares down at me through narrowed eyelids. "What evil are you conjuring?"

I look at him in puzzlement. "Brother, of what do you speak? Conjuring evil? Of course that has nothing to do with what I've been about or what my beloved and I intend for you or any of the brothers. I care for you all and would never want to harm you. Your kindness has made me tender for this family of brothers."

"Ah, so you see. It is only because of our kindness that you do not mean to destroy us. But I know. I know, it is not your nature to be kind, is it? Do not deny it. You must know. The night sky declared it. Evil was being done by you and this… this Other as you call him. Who else would be at the root of it? You must be at the source of it." He paces from the fire to the narrow cross-shaped opening in the wall at the far end of his cell.

His agitation unsettles me. I am a blade of grass against his rock of resistance. He berates me, twists the wrist of his brown cloak in his hands, and looks around as if hoping to discover some other proof for his frustration. I back against the wall and wish for some shield, some protection from the violence I feel coalescing within him, ready to be set against me.

"Where lurks he? Where is this Other now?

"I do not understand," I protest. "He is not here."

"You are not to see him again." The brothers lingering near the door steal away and out of sight at these words crashing like frozen ice columns.

"You cannot forbid me."

"I must and I shall. I will not dismiss you from your responsibilities to the brothers."

"How can you keep me from one of my own kind, from someone who is dear to me as family?"

"We are your family. We care for you. Without us, you would have died. We have brought you closer to the Lord and safe from the baser nature of your kind."

"Baser nature? Let us speak of which kind has a baser nature. I have known nothing but destruction at the hands of others like you. And when you brought me in from the shore, I was not dead. I was not at risk of any harm. I could have drifted in my sea cocoon for years. And for a long time, I often wished you had not brought me back into this consciousness. But now—now that I have found my beloved—I am filled with such gratitude to have arrived here. Even more—to have been brought here. Certainly that could have something to do with your god, even?"

"Be still." The ashen shadow over his face gives way to crimson, and then his skin turns translucent, as if he is about to wretch. In the slant light his face becomes luminous. "I sense it. Evil comes this way, and you have opened the space through which it shall pass unto us."

"Brother, do not speak so. I do not bring evil to us. Yargis and I do not mean harm, and we do not bring harm to you or any of the brothers." I want to weep, but hold my voice steady and look at him without fear. Brother Angus flinches when I use my beloved's name. "Yes, he has a name. Yargis has dwelled in seclusion and secret from you for many seasons, and he has not done you or the others any harm. Do you not think if he was evil or had anything to do with causing harm, he would have done so by now? Long ago?"

But Brother Angus shakes his head.

"You shall restrict yourself to our settlement. You shall keep to yourself. You will not leave, and he will not be permitted to enter."

"I do not understand why you would do this." I begin to weep.

"I do not care."

"Then I take my leave." When I turn and start for the entrance to his cell, he clutches the back of my cloak and turns me around to face him "And survive how? The two of you. Out there? He lives now only because of your kindness, the fragments of good will possible in your kind."

"He has dwelt near you successfully for a generous time. And I have been with him for a long passage, and we have been well and content. We do not just survive, but thrive."

I peel his hands off of me and pull myself up to my full height to stand a good head and shoulders above him. "We are of a race older than you and yours. We are bound by strengths you cannot comprehend."

"Oh, no. The contrary. I am only beginning to understand how profound the differences are. You are not God's Orphan. You have no comprehension of God. You are a base creature. An abomination. An error of nature…"

"But you always profess your god does not commit errors."

"I see now that Our Lord always intended your destruction, but somehow, somehow you and this other have persevered. I see it now. I am to make certain you do not procreate. God always eventually eliminates, washes away what is wrong. And I will be His agent in this circumstance."

"This is how you see me?" I whisper through my tears. The vile essence of his hatred leaves no room for air to move in the cell. It is hard for me to breathe.

"You will do as I tell you."

"I will do as I must. And what I must do is leave here."

He lifts a hand as if to strike me. I take a step back and hold out a hand ready to strike him back. He takes a step back and drops his hand, his shoulders curving in a sudden weariness.

"My dreams these many last nights have been filled with blood. Foretold by what I saw across the moon that night I found the two of you. You bring a nightmare upon us all. I was wrong to bring you within our gathering. I have not been vigilant. My inattention has allowed this to happen. Whatever your race, you are a woman, and as such you are the root of this corruption."

My mouth goes dry as a torment courses through my body.

A clump of peat falls and flares in the fire pit, overturning a clay pot of steaming fennel and moss balanced there. The pot's contents spill. The glowing fire smolders and hisses. The noise alters the tension in the air. Brother Angus flinches and looks around as if released from some dark place and now finds the room washed in light. He turns aside and places an open palm against his chest as if to still his heart, his hand a fluttering leaf.

"Please, Rehsotis. Do not persist in being with him. It will not end well."

"By forbidding it, you have secured it."

In silence we stand transfixed by what could be said next.

Outside, the wind shifts into a moan. The prayer bell begins to ring into the gloaming. Its iron tones seem far away, sped away from us upon the north wind.

"I have warned you," Brother Angus says at last.

"The brothers wait for you." The words are like stones from my mouth, and I walk out through the doorway from his cell and make my way to mine.

I remain with the brothers through the night and into the next day, but do not leave my chamber. I do not believe Brother Angus will truly harm us, but I know he is dismayed by what he witnessed between Yargis and me in his dreamscape.

My ache for my beloved is greater than any sense of caution. It does not matter to me what befalls us, as long as we are together. I bundle together my few belongings, wrap myself in a dark cloak, and walk into the rapidly chilling air of evening. A few of the brothers lift their hands in farewell. Others turn and close the door of their small huts against me and stay contained with their unfounded fears. I leave the monastery and make my way to Yargis's den.

* * *

I return to the sea-banked den. The robes on his sleeping pallet are flung over, as if he had just risen from resting and will return soon, carrying with him some shellfish or a gathering of wood to feed the embers in the fire pit. I drop my pack upon a flat stone used as a table and curl upon the pallet and wait. The wind calms. The rush of waves below comforts. Dozing, thoughts about another evening of salty caresses and embraces drift through my mind. My eyes close and I settle into a tidal sleep full of chambered dreams—but the dreams are too smooth, for they are void of murmurs from Yargis's thoughts. In my dreams I cast myself into one blue room after another but hear nothing of him. No echo. No call. When I awake, I am depleted.

I rise and move through air thickened with the realization that Yargis is gone. My thoughts turn to sand. I want to believe he has taken his small sea craft into the night and is already near the land

69

just beyond the edge of the sea. I want to believe that there he will ready a place for the two of us, enlarge the craft, and return for me. Certainly he knows what happened at the monastery. He tracked my encounter with his own sharp mind, and I have been too distracted and overwrought to find his reassurances.

For several days I trust in this. And in my longing, I weep. I tremble. I wait. I dwell in the cave for several weeks. My grief for Yargis increases. With my grief, something else increases within me.

I am with child.

* * *

I come to the place where I must write of her. I must write of my daughter.

No day passes in which I do not think of her.

She is complete, whole, and mine. Brother Angus and his god cannot claim her or diminish her.

She and I will not allow it.

As she rolls and flourishes within me, the realization that Yargis is not going to return intensifies. Too many nights of seeking him in my dreams pass in which there is nothing upon which to rest, nothing resonating of his thought or breath or heart to draw me to some understanding of where he journeyed or why. And without that compass point, I am rendered powerless. If I leave, I might arrive at a place more dangerous, and encounter others with treacherous hearts. The brothers, I know. Despite Brother Angus' harsh words, my instinct to protect my unborn child drives me to return to the monastery. I rationalize how they know me, and most will be even welcoming. And so, I return to the brothers. Brother Angus does not speak of our encounter. He hardly speaks to me at all. He only nods. I return to my hut. I resume my work.

* * *

At night, after banking the fires and planning for the next day, I curl within the warmth of my hut and sing to my unborn child, talk to her of Yargis, and the strong line of her ancestors. I enter her dreams. She enters mine. We fold around each other in our shared sleep, and I find comfort and warmth in the spiral of gestation—a weaving of images of my mother pleased and peaceful, of myself refined and embellished. I make plans for after my child's birth, when I will take her far from the Island of the Brothers, to a warmer place where vines, flowers, and fruit grow vibrant and lush. She fills me with these sorts of hopes. She is sanctuary for me. I delight in her presence, her movement in my womb, strong and dancing, her certain twirl beneath my heart.

One night, in my dream, I am suspended in an amber liquid, deep in an undersea cavern, a golden light high above me. I am being pulled down deeper into the liquid, and I fear I will not survive the descent, yet I am riveted by the beauty of what I see around me. Within arm's reach is a red, striated velvet wall, pleated with crannies and tucked with small, richly hued clutches of blossoms—cinnabar touched by shades of blue, luminous greens streaked with yellow—each bloom more tempting and intense than the previous, one after the other around and along the sea wall. But despite the beauty surrounding me, I fear I am going too deep, too far from the surface, and that soon I will drown.

Then from within and all around me, I hear a loving entreaty: "Don't be afraid. Just breathe." I know it is the voice of the child I carry.

"Be in repose," she says. "I am here. I am well, and I love you. I want you to see my world as it is now."

I do just as she tells me. I take a breath, and the warm amber liquid fills and passes through my lungs as easy as air, even easier. In my dream, I am within my own womb, and even more, I am looking through my daughter's eyes. For this time, we occupy an internal, shared sea. We swim and dive and move with open arms and long-legged ease within the expanse of a growing self.

Of all the dreams I have created, occupied, or altered, this is the one dream from which I never want to awaken. Both of us so present and lovely to each other. My daughter's gift to me: The sensation of grace. The motion of spirit. Distilled forgiveness and selfless love. For myself. For Grendel, certainly. Yenheth, absolutely. A grace my daughter receives from her father, now incarnate within me.

When she presses deep into the widespread joints of my hips, I know she is ready to arrive. The brothers have suspected nothing during the entire pregnancy. Brother Angus attributes my slower step to the lingering sadness and loneliness for Yargis. Although I still long for him, it becomes tenderly more bearable with each month of her increasing presence in my body. As her mark and manner became more deliberate and clear, what could have seemed a futile or even cruel passage gained meaning and purpose.

She transcends Yargis and me; she compels and propels me forward. As her weight in my body increases, I find myself attending to all of my daily duties with increasing tenderness. My daughter's imminent arrival sustains me through the days of preparing food, clearing the brothers' tables for their work, spreading out the thin sheets of gold leaf, grinding and mixing the dyes and powders for their paints. From a small brass box, embellished with a setting of amber, I remove a small ball of ultramarine, distilled and blended by my own hand from finely ground lapis lazuli, a little honey, and wax. I know this will be the color of her eyes.

My body is a new landscape, a detail of the terrain never before witnessed on the Island of the Brothers, thickened by my daughter's insistence. My spirit lightens. I even sing as I work—songs I thought forgotten rise from within me, sonorous and ripe with the images of the Anathian in our prime. The brothers find me approachable in my ease. During the long passage of time in my state of expectancy, even the tension between Brother Angus and me is eased by the quiet of routine.

* * *

I know nothing of what to expect when she decides to arrive in the outer world. The elders and Yenheth sometimes shared with me stories about how Grendel and I were born. They told me that for days the elders fed the communal fire with sage and ginger. With mortar and pestle, they created aromatic pastes from figs and rosemary to massage into Yenheth's temples. They rubbed her back, arms, and legs with oil infused with pepper and lavender—a fragrance for comfort and energy. Yenheth rolled onto her hands and knees and panted, then rested, curled around the tribe's birthing stone—a stone of soft marble from an island far away in distance and time. She let others bring her to her feet and walked the circumference of the common room, the fire glowing and warm. Several times she walked the Labyrinth, and the spirits in the stone sang and chanted blessings. After many days, the sun seemed to tear open the roof of the common house, for light filled the chamber. Yenheth fell to her hands and knees, but she did not cry out. Instead, she laughed. Her waters opened and drenched her in a florid-smelling fluid and the elders near her called out in adulation and joy. Slowly, she crawled her way to a far corner of the chamber where thick violet-colored robes were suspended from the racks to the ground, creating a room apart from the open hall. Cushions and honey-colored fleeces covered the floor and dozens of shell lamps glowed on ledges and around the room. Two of the elders joined Yenheth behind the thick tapestries. She crouched, closed her eyes, and with her mouth wide open and arms wrapped around an elder's hips, she howled—one long sustained call that carried my brother and me through centuries and forward to the moment in which we arrived. And an elder knelt and reached over Yenheth, and she fell silent into her breath. The elder gathered my brother into her arms and gently offered him to Yenheth—a son—his arms already reaching out, his legs stretched full length, his eyes amber in the shining light.

Then my mother Yenheth cried out again, and I slipped into the world.

I was unexpected.

Twin births were very rare in the Tribe of Anath. No arms were ready to greet me. The elders explained that because I was tucked so well behind my brother, even they could not sense my presence. Our hearts beat in such well-hinged synchronicity, one could not be discerned from the other. Gathering me from the curls of the fleece upon which I fell, an elder cradled me gently. "Here—another," she said to Yenheth. "A daughter, as well."

"A sister for the brother," my mother Yenheth said. "A sign that he will have many following him."

* * *

As my daughter begins to press down to gain hard entry into this world, I wonder if I am the first to ever make this passage without another of my kind as helpmate. I prepare myself. There soon will be the days when the tidal press and release will consume my body. I decide it will be better to be away from the brothers; the act of birth will terrify them, that some new horror forces its way into their midst. Even more, I want to be as near as possible, in memory at least, to Yargis. This time I leave a note of my intentions: *I must be away for a time. Do not be afraid.*

In the cover of night, I return to the grotto I shared with my beloved, and find it as I left it, stocked with some provisions, the walls covered with carved comforts: his bow, his lute, several flutes, drums, and warm robes. The lamps are all at least half-full of oil. I set them all alight with a spark from his burning glass and build a fire. In the midst of my daughter's gripping possession of my body, I make a hot brew from black cohosh and skullcap and sip it from one of Yargis' earthenware mugs. Clutching his cape around me, I rock through the labor and watch as the sky above the sea turns dark and fills with stars.

She takes her time to become part of the external world. It feels as if she will tear through my abdomen or pull out the thread of my spine and emerge on a wash of vivid rose foam from my core. I spread my legs wide but do not believe I can accommodate her passage.

She drives her rhythm out through each doorway to my body—my mouth, eyes, ears, groin. I plunge into our effort to find each other until my legs and arms tingle, then burn, then go numb as if filled with lead. It reminds me of how it felt ages ago in the vineyards of my tribe, where I helped drill and drive poles to support the grapevines, lifting again and again the post driver. Or how it feels when I climb the path from the cove to the crest of the skellig again and again without stopping. With each breath, my daughter becomes more present, her safe passage more likely secure.

How I yearn for Yargis. To have him near—to be able to reach out and hold onto him, to look upon him and into the sea-green comfort of his eyes, to measure my own breath against his. I want to hear his voice against my ear whispering, *All is well,* and to be wrapped by his love. I hold the burning glass in my hand, stare into its undulating colors, and seek his image. Instead, amid a glimmering purple light bursting from the burning glass, I find a quiet place created by her and by me together.

In her face—such wisdom and certainty—her father.

Impatience and curiosity—her mother.

All answers and riches reside within this new being.

She trembles like lute strings vibrating with her father's heartbeat and pulsing with my blood. I wrap her within Yargis' cloak and curl with her upon the pallet he and I shared, where she was most likely conceived. I place water, mead, and small bowls of herbs to be within easy reach. The chords of my balance and bearing are struck and strummed by her small and perfect hands. In my arms I hold perfection distilled. The night parts to reveal her first dawn, and my daughter and I move from purple to gray to a rain-slicked green morning, delighted with each other.

No elders chant.

No mother, sister, or elder daughter holds attendance.

No lover glitters with enchantment.

Just my infant and this new being I have become—*mother.*

In my arms, she finds a breast and suckles with an amazing insistence. She does not falter. She cries out for the world and insists that I rejoin it. I find the wonders of the universe in the crease of her eyelids, the dimples of her hands, the flex and arch of her feet. Can she know the wonderment she holds for me? As I carry her from our insulated cocoon into the larger world, I encounter my own self, renewed. When I study her face, inhale her exhalations, I realize I will risk or sacrifice everything to keep her safe, to keep her whole. I call out to my ancestors, to the women of Anath, and ask for her name. As luminous and full as a pearl, in one breath, I speak it for the first time:

Illisante. Yenheth's granddaughter.
Illisante. Yargis' daughter.
Illisante. The promise for the Anathian.
Again and again, I sing her name.
Illisante. My daughter.

* * *

The short hours of light at that time of year pour through the angled opening to our cave and dapple our den blue and amber. The sea lifts its wave lullabies and these rest easy and generous upon our ears. I float in the violet swirl of Illisante's eyes. She gazes at me with mutual adoration. We are whole unto each other. I move and turn around her as if she were my axis. She nurses deep and often and presses herself into me until we become an inseparable and continuous interior landscape. My contentment seeps into our mutual dreaming. I am cheered and strengthened. With each breath, I grieve for Yargis and his not being present with us, and at the same time, I yearn for him less.

At first I do not notice how she does not grow. She strikes an equilibrium with me, within herself, and rests at that constant. Months pass, and days fill with the same identical rhythms. We occupy a rarified dimension of the world and hang suspended in time, neither of us changing. Neither of us moves in any direction that would take us away from each other.

* * *

The sunrise brands the morning edge of the horizon, and the sun surfaces from salted mist wavering with promise. I hold Illisante in my lap as we sit on the rock ledge high above the sea. We watch a sea tern flit and turn in the air, higher and higher until it dips and swoops, again and again in a mirror dance with the waves. She makes her zagging way farther and farther from us.

Someone moves along the slip of beach below. My heart turns for just a moment when I think it could be Yargis. Then my eyes focus and I recognize two silhouettes. Brothers Galweth and Patrick climb the narrow stone outcrops that crisscross the cliff face up to us. We remain motionless when they finally come to kneel next to us.

"We have been worried. We have been looking for you. We feared that, considering your burden, harm had come to you."

I shake my head. "No harm. Nothing like that at all."

Brother Patrick touches the edge of the cloak folded upon Illasante's forehead. "I would have hoped you would have told me. I guessed it was something like this."

Brother Galweth is braver and rests a gentle thumb against Illisante's forehead. "Come back to us. You and…"

"Illisante. My daughter."

He nods. "It would be the best thing for you both."

Brother Patrick reaches to take her from me, but when I hold her tight against my shoulder, he instead helps me to get to my feet.

"Wait here." I carry her with me into the den and set her dozing upon a cushion while I gather some of what I hold most dear into a satchel, including a small alabaster lamp, a set of goblets, several pouches of herbs, an ash wood lute, and two flutes carved from bone. Illisante still sleeps when I nest her into a sling and take up the satchel. The four of us then make our way up the rest of the cliffside to the gorse-choked pathway.

At first the brothers stand apart with caution as they watch Illisante and me move into their midst. They come closer to her daily, and begin to greet her with gentle voices.

She awakes each morning with bright eyes, soft caresses, and gentle murmurs for me. After dressing her and wrapping her into a warm, wool-lined sling, she rides upon my hip throughout the days as I repeat my daily rhythm tending the brothers. From her hip perch, she smiles and trills when one or another of the brothers dote on her. Soon they all treat her as something like a pet: One brings a piece of their midday bread to her, smeared with rose hip jelly; another lifts her from my shoulder and carries her into the thawing garden, explaining to her what we would soon grow there, and she nods as if in understanding; another brings a smooth piece of driftwood, upon which he carved half- moons and star shapes for her delight.

Seasons pass, yet Illisante does not change. She remains the same as the day we returned from Yargis' den. She does not grow. She does not complain. We read each other's gestures like music and call and respond to each other with the brothers to add to our improvisation —their deep voices drawing her midnight blue gaze. She humbles them. She only protests when I set her to rest at night, when for a few brief moments, she rails at the gloaming, and does not rest until I sing her songs gentle and soft into her shell-shaped golden ears.

One morning following midwinter's new moon, she rolls into me at dawn, but does not nurse. Her hands stroke my cheek, my neck, and my shoulder. Her eyes open, then close just as if she drifted into a dream. I close my own eyes and try to follow her into that internal expanse. But this time, the gossamer-draped dance of her dreams does not open to partner with me. I cannot track her and cannot find her. When the light fills our chamber full of morning, and our shadows blend against the interior wall, my daughter inhales, gasps, gives out a soft cry, and calls out one glittering word: "*Rehsotis.*" Then she stops breathing. She slips away. She is gone.

* * *

78

I go mad. Inside the dark moon of grief, I wail and weep. I search for her spirit and enlist all my powers to move my soul to find where hers strums. Time swallows me. Within its hollow limitless belly, I cannot track it. I want to turn inside out and find her still within me, expose her hiding place, as if she were playing some game of the womb.

Despair and terror converge.

Moonlight fills yet another evening and cuts bladed edges around Brother Angus when he appears at my chamber door. I confuse him at first for Yenheth and then with Grendel. Not until he speaks does my mind grind down into the present.

"Time for you to return to us." He calls to me again and again.

"She is not in this world. She is dead. Let me help you. May we help you?"

It is the only time Brother Angus asks for my permission. And because he offers the gift of a question, I receive and accept it.

For a long string of days, he feeds me and speaks in low drummed tones. Upon the thick bridge of his voice, I make my way back, a little, to my life and understand what I need to do next. I describe the oils and cloth used. I reveal the rituals not so much intended to preserve the shell of the body, but to comfort the living attending the body. He nods, says nothing, and leaves my side. When he returns, he presents oils and herbs approximating those I used after the death of Grendel and my mother Yenheth.

Together we minister to the dead body of Illisante.

"I had a sister. She was stubborn. In that way, you remind me of her." Brother Angus' voice is soft. His eyes are closed and he holds Illisante's lifeless hand.

"It still pains you?"

"She died in childbirth. And her daughter languished. Died within a fortnight."

"The father had abandoned her. Our parents were not kind to her. They could not feed another. Not during that time of famine. But I should have done more. I should have...perhaps I should have taken her away. Perhaps we could have done well enough on our own. Perhaps." He opens his eyes and gently tucks my daughter's small hand beneath the rough, butter colored swaddling. Just before he steps out of my hut, he turns and places a hand over his heart. "I have not been kind to you. Not as kind as you deserve."

* * *

The next night, beneath the light of the tentative waning moon, Brother Angus follows me as I hold her, strapped against my bosom, out of my chamber. The other brothers stand silent along the path we walk. Again I make my way to the sea, to the cliff side where Yargis and I dwelled, carrying the swaddled body of our daughter into the relentless sea wind, my mouth full of the names of my family, of her family. Brother Angus comes to stand behind me as I repeat their names again and again, stringing the names together into a lamentation: Chanan, Yenheth, Grendel, Yargis. At last, when the names are choked and twisted unrecognizable by my sobs, I release her into the waves.

And then Brother Angus offers up his own song of lamentation in his beloved Latin, and I let myself lean back and against him.

We watch the cocooned remains of my daughter Illisante roll and recede into the white-maned waves. Brother Angus touches my shoulder, as if in blessing. Then he leaves my side and in heavy cloaked steps makes his way up the cliffside and disappears over its crest. I stand, my vision affixed upon the space of sea where I last saw her until the sun rims the entire bell of sky velvet red, the red that marks all abundant beginnings and all astonishing endings. When the sun throbs high in the dome of day, I turn and climb past the entrance to the sea cave without stopping to look inside. I return to the brothers. I return, but nothing is the same.

The brothers do not look me in the eye. When they speak to me, they blanket their voices in uneasy comfort. Some touch a hand to my shoulder if we pass in a hall or along a pathway. But they do not look at me fully.

Years of quiet wash against the rock of my immovable and silent grief. No one says anything more of Yargis and Illisante, and the silt of my grief fills in the gaps of my life until all is choked, obscured, hidden.

* * *

With increasing frequency, the young men who arrive on the shore are not the golden sons full of promise for their family's advancement, but ailing children sent away in an attempt to hide them from the spread of the Dark Plague. The Smallheaded from the mainland believe the brothers and their prayers can save the lives of these many sons.

Brother Angus adds to my list of duties the preparation of corpses and graves.

Some of the brothers take small boats to minister to the ill on the mainland. With noble purposes they leave, usually at dawn, just after morning prayers. Layered in rough robes, the departing brothers carry satchels crammed with husks of brown bread, skins of honeyed wine, herbs, and oils. None of them return. We do not hear of any survivors.

Once the Island of the Brothers offered refuge to two hundred. Now there are fewer than fifty.

My own immunity to the Plague should challenge their long-held assumption of my inferior standing, but many avoid me even more and all seem suspicious of my continued health and strength.

* * *

I am turning loaves in the clay ovens the morning Brother Angus raps at the doorframe of the bakery hut where the ovens glow amber and blast warmth.

"Orphan, this is Brother Cloaved. He will be working with you for as long as he is able. Welcome him and be grateful." Brother Angus nods admittance to the bent and limping form of the Smallheaded leaning at his side.

"Welcome, Brother Cloaved." My voice cracks like a neglected book just opened.

His hood falls from his head as he turns toward my voice. Massed lumps of tufted gray and rusty knots of hair cover Brother Cloaved's head, his flat nostrils fold low upon his face, and thick lips roll down over an approximation of a chin. Puckered and angry scar tissue glistens across his generous forehead. Where eyes should be, it appears as if the sculptor pressed two thumbs into the clay and abandoned the work in frightened haste. Brother Cloaved is broader than he is tall, and he stands only up to my elbow. His uneven shoulders lift high around his neck. That his spine is severely twisted and knotted is evident through his thick tunic.

"May the Lord Our God bless you. Put me to work, you who they call Orphan. I must earn my place at your side." His voice halts my heart. The voice. Such a voice.

From his mangled body rises a calm and round-noted voice lean and true as a reed and deep as an autumn-burnished sunset. I hear the voice of what could be a god—a creator capable of fashioning all of us, Anathian and Smallheaded, with the kindest and most resolute heart.

"The Orphan is a creature we took in many years ago. We found her. Upon the shore. Abandoned by her kind. More than once. She will be a good teacher. Learn our habits and routine. You are suited to each other. I pray." Brother Angus snaps these words into the air, cracking the enchantment. His disdain baffles me.

Brother Cloaved reaches two enormous hands toward me, his fingers thick and round as turnips. I rest both my hands into his and he clasps them tightly, his skin warm, nearly hot. I sense no fear as his hands touch my skin's fine hair covering; I feel none toward him. Then he takes one of my hands into both of his and traces its contours as if he holds a fine cup.

"Such strength. You are very strong." He turns his head up to the ceiling and smiles.

"She is strong, that is true. Certainly much work awaits your attention. I will see you both at evensong." Brother Angus snaps. Cold air presses into the warmth of the chamber when he opens and shuts the door, but only briefly.

"I mean to work hard for the brothers," says Brother Cloaved.

"They will be grateful to have you in their midst. Their numbers dwindle."

"I do not think they want me in their midst, as you say. I think they want to tuck me away with you, Orphan. Can that be what you want to be called?"

This is a keen mind and I have not encountered such speed of wit in many years. Something once heavy in my chest eases a bit.

"That is not my name."

"What, then, may I call you?

"You may call me Rehsotis."

"Rehsotis. Rehsotis." He lifts my name with a gentle intake of breath and releases it with a tendrilled sigh.

"Supper approaches and we cannot keep the brothers waiting. How best shall I instruct you?" I examine his sightless face and misshapen form. He is not wearing shoes and his webbed toes are encased by calloused skin.

"There are many ways to understand and learn. Let me follow you as I best I can, and I will learn. Let me hold a sleeve and listen to your instructions. Guide my hands. I will learn."

In the firelight, we move as if joined by gentle threads, two beings in tandem. I guide his hands along the shelves and name each item as I take it down and prepare the evening meal. We create an amiable dance from pot to table, a convivial cadence in the tearing and stacking of bread. With each task a well-seasoned and gentle patience deepens. His hand rests over mine through the steps of grinding the grain and seeds into coarse flour, and with shared instinct, we stop just before the flour melts into pulverized paste. He learns to milk the goats with one lesson. He does not complain about the incessant churning demanded of butter. And so I enter the safe harbor of Brother Cloaved's friendship. As we work together, we talk with each other. Not one at the other—but the gift of true conversation. He'll dissect one of the stories he has heard from the Smallheaded's holy texts, often wondering about its veracity.

"I mean, truly, to live within a fish as Jonah did? Clearly the writer of that tale never experienced the interior of a fish—gigantic or otherwise."

He pauses from stirring a steaming stew.

"Do you voice these doubts with the others? Is not such a line of questioning forbidden? My understanding is that all is of your god, from your god, for your god. Is there room for error in that formula?" I feel myself smirking.

Brother Cloaved lets loose a walloping chortle. "Ha, you are right with that, my friend. So right with that. These are what I've come to think of as 'Rehsotis Thoughts.' I can tell you these things,and know that we will talk all through and about them. And you do not condemn me."

"Of course I do not condemn you. I think you are always entirely correct."

He hoots as he presses his weight into a bowl of brown, fermenting bread. "If my father could hear that. Convinced I was a demon. And with our living so removed from any hamlet, he managed to keep me hidden away for a good many years. One night I heard him berating my mother. Yelled at her that I was the result of her having cavorted with an incubus, he did. He made her weep as often as he could. Dear woman. Couldn't bear it. And so, when I was still a lad, she secreted me away to the nearest monastery. Couldn't bear to see her go, but she insisted I would find a safe shelter. She was right, I imagine. And it was there that Brother Angus came one day and told me of this place."

"I am glad-hearted that you decided to journey here." I pause in decanting golden mead. "In such a short while, you have me feeling comforted. I look forward to years in your company."

His voice graces my ear. He wraps each story in a sonorous incantation of goodness. He calls the ceaseless island wind "music from heaven's flute." He sings with it and steps into easy harmony with each lifting shift of air moaning through the stars. He accompanies the grieving, groaning waves. And he laughs at the rain—laughter having nothing to do with a mean spirit, but a simple, well-rooted joy in the creation.

We settle into a gentle rhythm of our own world. Before dawn, Brother Cloaved makes his way to my cell's door and calls to me, his voice turning my name into a silver bell. We weave our way through our chores with steadfast ease. He leaves to attend prayers and against their lingering echoes, returns to share the work of whatever chores occupy us. The brothers seem relieved to leave us to ourselves. We become nearly invisible to them.

* * *

The dream crashes into a night after I begin to feel centered in a quieted, meditative life. Its images flash bright, searing open the curtain between my own and another dreamer's deep-sleep world. The other dreamer catches sight of me at their once night-locked door and slams it shut. The image reverberates enough to bring me awake. It contains Brother Cloaved, the generous and now well-loved features of his face twisted in panic and pain, a cry frozen upon his great lips. It occurs to me he must be ill and unable to call for me, so I pull my cloak on and hurry to his chamber. The full moon illuminates the center yard, the cross in sharp shadow before me, marking an enormous dark path.

At Cloaved's cell, I call out his name and rap at the door. From within comes a muffled cry and thud. Now certain he is in distress, I open the door without hesitation. As the door opens, a dark figure pushes me down, scrambles over me, and runs out into the yard. My forehead strikes the threshold, and for a moment I cannot see. I turn to watch a tall figure flee around the far wall of the Common Hall. I call out to Brother Cloaved, and from a corner I hear him weeping. I crawl to him and find him, washed now in moonlight from the gaping door, naked and lying upon his stomach, his mouth gagged, wrists and ankles bound together with leather straps. First I cover him. Then I try for as much gentleness as possible with my shaking hands as I pull the straps away and tug the gag of cloth from his throat. His released howls rush into the night, a torrent of agony. Silent and strong, I hold him. He tells me nothing, but weeps without ceasing until dawn when he falls into a whimpering sleep. After covering him with several warm robes, I slip away and rush to tell Brother Angus.

Without a word to any other, Brother Angus follows me to Brother Cloaved's chamber. Brother Angus kneels next to my friend and with a soft voice at his ear whispers, "Dear Brother, what has been done to you?"

"Nothing." His voice contains no music. It is flat as stone.

"Dear Brother, tell me who did this to you, and I shall put him out." With this, Brother Angus rests a long hand upon the older man's forehead.

Brother Cloaved shakes his head with slow certainty. "I shall not. Even more, I cannot. I do not know him."

"But I must do something. Let me do something for you."

"For the time, let me dress and then permit me to stay with Rehsotis."

Brother Angus. "I do not want to stay in this chamber. Please let me stay in the protection of my friend for a while."

Brother Angus leans back, his brow furrowed. "I cannot imagine why…" Tears stream down Brother Cloaved's terraced cheeks. "Well yes, then. Very well. Yes, I can understand. You should not be alone."

Sometime later, Brother Angus asks me to see if I can discover who violated Brother Cloaved. On numerous nights of dark sleep, I try to retrieve the answer from Brother Cloaved's dreams. But his will is strong. Despite my dream-gliding skill and the degree of trust I share with him, nothing of the truth ever drifts into my view. During our time together during the day, I do not ask, even though I share Brother Angus' desire to rid the Island of the Brothers of the one who enacted such cruelty upon a gentle soul.

Brother Cloaved never returns to his chamber; I unroll his pallet next to mine and from that day he dwells with me. He does not leave my side. He never sings again. And he never speaks of that night.

In time, he again tells his stories with warmth as we work ground oats and flax seed into loaves. He asks me to sing one of our favorite songs as we work the gardens. He collects shells from the sea and with thick mud plaster, covers the interior of our chamber with their whorled and spun beauty. He does not hurry, and it pleases him.

* * *

According to the Calendar of the Brothers, Brother Cloaved dies in his sleep on the Eve of the Epiphany. They have no idea how long I have been braced for the inevitable event. I hear him take in a long and staggering gasp, utter "My Creator! I am here," and then… silence. I light every candle and lamp in our chamber. I prepare him for his final journey as if he were one of the Anathian—I press salt and oil into his dear old and deformed joints, sing and pray so low and soft that only he and I, and the spirits around us, can hear. His spirit hovers near and around me throughout the darkest hours. Somewhere in that time, in the satin stitch between night and dawn, I hear Brother Cloaved singing. At last I hear him singing again. His voice surrounds me and takes me into a place full of warmth and amber. It makes me feel stronger than I have felt in ages, and the strength works upon my chest like a thaw. With invigorated breath, I can let him go. He can now be golden and wonderful in all ways, his own illuminated manuscript.

Upon morning light, I tell Brother Angus about Brother Cloaved's death. Four of the novices come into our hut and carry his linen-wrapped form into their chapel. During their prayers for his soul and final passage, I cannot stop thinking that standing among the brothers is the man who silenced Brother Cloaved's greatest grace and gift.

The desire to be away from the Island of the Brothers and on to another place reawakens, even as the echoes of prayer in the chapel fades. I ache to search for Yargis, or any other of my tribe.

* * *

When Brother Angus returns from the mainland from what he calls "a gathering of souls," he does not drink his mead or eat his goat cheese with the same ravenous energy of the past. He does not bring any recruits with him, and soon he excuses himself to his chamber, saying he is too ill to tend to prayers or lessons

I take herbed broth to him and mean to leave the warm clay mug at his bedside and steal away, but he asks me to stay

"The recurring fever is decimating entire settlements."

We can hear the seed-tight tones of the brothers chanting just below our feet.

"I found entire families stretched out where they died in their huts. The neglected stock lay dead and bloated in their holding pens. Packs of wild dogs and emboldened wolves scratched and tore at the remains. And the carrion crows—always the crows. They swooped over me, watchful, expectant." His low and hollow voice fills his chamber with shadow.

A few days later, I find Brother Angus collapsed at the back of the chapel. He does not want to be taken to his hut, but I am stronger and prevail. I minister to him, alone. The others hover near the entrance of his dwelling, asking me if they could be of assistance, relieved when I assure them all Brother Angus needs are their prayers. Their sense of compassion for their leader is not stronger than their fear or sense of self-preservation.

He does not let me touch the lumps swelling on his neck and along his arms. Soon after turning the color of charred wood, they split like an overripe fig, releasing the yeasty, dark scent of vinegar. Blood streaks his water. He burns with fever and cries out to his god. And amid his collecting madness, while still able to find the language he needs, he confesses what I both want and do not want to hear.

"I witnessed it." He breathes, lips swollen and blistered.

"Witnessed what?" I clasp his thrashing hands so he cannot tear at his burning skin.

"He came to me."

"Who came to you?" My voice is soft, for I do not want to disturb the spell of comfortable understanding. It does not matter. I cannot speak with enough gentleness to shift the pressure of his intent.

"Yargis. Your Yargis." Bloodied spittle gathers at the corners of his mouth. He turns his deep-green eyes upon me, and they burn with lamplight intensity upon me through the contrast of blood-rimmed lids.

"Yargis?"

Brother Angus nods, and grasps my hands as tightly as I grasp his. "In the cover of a moonless night, he came to me, asking that the brothers would continue to protect and keep safe his beloved Rehsotis, but that he needed to leave, could not take you with him. He knew—even then he knew you carried Illisante."

"But why? Why did he need to leave?"

He falls back upon his pallet, his breath rattling wet and rapid. For a few moments, he babbles a string of Latin prayers unfamiliar to me. He continues to look at me, and I search his eyes for some answer; he draws his face closer to mine, and I expect he will tell me more, but now his words are choked and muffled by rising phlegm in his chest.

During his last days, he recognizes no one. In a few final moments of clear voice, his words are a mangled collection of memorized prayers and catechism.

With his last exhalation, he murmurs, "*Veni, lumen cordium.*"

In the prayer-paused hours after his death, the brothers gather stones for his grave and dig a shallow pit not too far from the cross at the skellig's summit. I take down from our chamber wall an old tapestry of a tree redolent with ripe pomegranates—the one he told me his mother gave to him just before he left his family's village—and swaddle his prepared body within it.

The brothers hoist his body from his pallet onto a ceremonial travois which is processed into the chapel. They pray and chant from sunset until the next dawn, when we all accompany his body to the shallow burial pit where we cover it over with gray and ragged stones. By midday, the dome of his grave reaches just above my head. Without another word, we trail away from his grave. I walk to the edge of the skellig and watch the sun fall upon the shoulders of the next day.

* * *

The most recent storm is short, with snow more of air and mist than flint and ice, gracing all larch limbs and reaching reeds with a crystalline sheath. The earliest of buds now ache for release from ice cases. The sky high in gray white light magnifies and then shatters all sound against the hillsides. The owls call to the approaching spring, and the larch and willow lean into their insistent fugues.

Matters of transition and the shift in hierarchy occupy the brothers and they try to ignore the shifting season and the reversal of the prevailing winds. The light pleats fuller and long against the kneeling stone near Brother Angus' grave than even three moons ago. But I am restless. During the night, I find myself caught in the strange dreams of some approaching force. At daybreak my body aches as if I had been running in my sleep. An unfamiliar panic increases each morning as I fill the brothers' midday bowls with their brown bread, boiled onions, leeks and lovage.

During a bright and shining midday, I tend the gardens with Brothers Galweth and Patrick. They bicker with good intent about who best might lead the Brotherhood forward. Brother Patrick wants someone devoted to more time making illuminated copies of the manuscript.

"The work of illumination needs to continue, I agree." Brother Galweth leans toward Brother Patrick and brushes garden soil from his apron. "But we need to think of what needs to be done to keep ourselves well and whole. And we have more youth arriving in need of tending and comfort.

"But it is only through devotion to the manuscript that we leave a true mark. What good are ceaseless days of prayer or devotion? We can live on bread and water and glorify the Creator with the work. We must deny our worldly cravings and fold ourselves into the passion of the blood of Christ." Brother Patrick plunges his sod pick into the dense earth with increasing vehemence.

Brother Galweth stands up from his portion of the garden and watches his companion, then shakes his head. "I do not think denying our hunger for more than bread will lead to anything other than a settlement of even fewer."

The wind shifts and wraps our cloaks tight around us as if to make us warm. A sea bird skims close to us, its shriek alarming by its unexpected nearness. With its cry, we stand and lean back to watch its angled ascent. We trace its white wing-bladed route out above the dark sea and toward the horizon, and there we see them—the red sails. I call out in alarm as sharp and surprising as the sea bird's. Brothers Galweth and Patrick look at me and then again at the red glints at the edge of the world.

"Not good. Not good, my brothers. Other Smallheaded approach and these are not like you."

"Slow, slow, dear Orphan. What do you mean? Smallheaded?"

Brother Galweth clasps my arm and looks out at the sea with me. "Who are they? I have not seen such a colored sail. How many are there? I see two, six, twelve. Are there twelve?" Brother Patrick's voice grows louder as he counts.

"They are of your race, but from far shores. They are not concerned with matters of the manuscript or your view of the Lord your God. They listen and believe in stories of gods more like monsters who are driven for their own gain, and they use those stories as a reason to take all, use all, claim all—for themselves."

"How can you be certain? Do they not come as pilgrims?" Brother Galweth's optimism still holds.

"Brother—pilgrims do not come in such numbers." Brother Patrick turns to face these signs. "Why are there so many?"

"Because they know they cannot be stopped in such numbers. I know these boats. Each carries at least fifty of their kind. Their crafts are lean and swift. Their minds are dull but determined. You must prepare. They will not value your true worth." My sobs choke and dull the words. I hurry from the brothers to the monastery's enclosure. Brothers Galweth and Patrick rush close behind me.

"Yes. She is right. The boats draw toward us with speed. Already I see the full edges of their sails. Clear and growing. You counted true, Brother. Twelve ships. If she foretells rightly, six hundred are carried toward us." Brother Galwest overtakes me as he cries out these words and hurries to his comrades gathering for evening prayers.

"Six hundred, at least. You must hide all you do not want them to claim. They will raid first, then decide what to steal. If I am wrong, so much the better. I would like to be proven wrong in this regard. But take my caution to heart. Make haste. You have but hours."

Their eyes widen as they look to me and then back to the sea. I speak so rarely, my words rend their walls of restraint. They rush after me, dropping their hoes and chisels along the path. We hasten to the monastery, all of us calling out warnings, urging everyone to gather their fine and treasured works.

As if of the same mind, all the brothers cluster around us and listen with open mouths to what we know approaches the shore. Without hesitation, all turn and speed to the library, store huts, and their own dwellings to collect all they can in baskets and satchels, then gather at the chapel doorway.

"I know of a safe place. Follow me." With those words I lead the band of brothers to the leeward side of the skellig hidden and farthest from the arriving Smallheaded. At the cliff edge above Yargis' chamber, the birth chamber of my daughter Illisante, we cast down knotted, thick coils, and with treasures slung and strapped to their backs, the brothers descend with me to the sea cave's entrance. When the treasures and provisions are set safe into the cave, Brothers Galweth and Patrick pull up the ropes and scramble down to join us, rocks and stones falling before them and into the sea. With a grace and speed made smooth by decades of living alongside each other, we fill the cave with bundles of carvings, books, icons, and relics. We encircle the firepits with baskets of kelp-wrapped cheeses, rounds of heavy bread, and jugs of mead and beer. When the last of what we carried is tucked into place, I pull several robes from Yargis' pallet; and beneath the protection and warmth they once offered to my lover and me, I shield stacks of the brothers' manuscripts—a mere fractioned whisper of decades of their patient scribing and tender brushstrokes.

While I do this, my thoughts center on Brother Cloaved, and I murmur blessings for my dear friend's memory, for the warm days he offered, and the understanding of his gifts to me. I invoke incantations for protection of all arranged in the cave. The brothers take up the chant in their own manner, in their own way. Together we finish arranging the coverings, tucking the treasures into safe ledges and crannies, then we stand back to survey what we have hidden.

"Very good. And now I take your leave." Brother Galweth pulls his hood over his head and makes the sign of the cross before the brother makes his way to the cave opening.

"Where are you going? We are safe here. We can wait until they find the settlement deserted and leave." The brothers plead with him and protest his exit.

"Think, my brothers. If these invaders come upon our dwellings left in tumbled evidence of a hasty abandonment, they will imagine we are hiding and search for us. If they meet with me, I will tell them how I sent you away. I will tell them there is nothing to value or claim."

"They will torture you. You cannot reason with these Smallheaded." I grasp his elbow and stop him before he steps out of the cave.

"No tortuous twist conceived by their wrinkled minds will draw forth your place of sanctuary." Brother Galweth's voice is certain as granite.

"You are right. And so is God's Orphan. I will come with you." Brother Patrick joins his closest brother and no one doubts his purpose. "I join you."

"And so I." One by one, the brothers take steps toward their two fellows of the keenest vision.

Brother Galweth looks from one to another and at last upon me. "They are keen and greedy, Brother. I know this. If they find many of you there and you demonstrate the thin manner in which you lived, they might well leave without searching and uncovering hints of our hiding place."

He nods in either agreement or resignation and turns to leave.

We scrabble up the cliff rock in a ragged line and make our way back to the settlement. The brothers gather in the chapel. Brother Galweth stands before them all. He raises his arms to begin their evensong, and as one and then another join in the brass-toned chant, they turn their faces up to their leader with cheeks made luminous by tears. For the first time since Brother Angus' death, their voices are steady and true. The chapel vibrates with the unified lift and turn of their voices.

As I listen to Brother Galweth line out the prayers to end the day, his voice full of heart and his open soul, the brothers breathe with increasing ease and trust.

It is time for me to leave. I believe the arriving Smallheaded will not find the brothers' rich paints, fragile leaves of gold, glorious books filled with their artful scripts, the elaborate carvings and metal work of their icons and reliquaries. Waiting for them instead is a clutch of simple dwellings, several immovable large stone crosses carved with inter-gripping patterns and creatures, and two-dozen unarmed and chanting men.

But they will not find me.

As Brother Galweth calls out his prayers, his face smoothed by his faith and belief in all manner of goodness, I move without word or sound out of the chapel, gather a sack of dry rusks from the kitchen and my belongings from my hut, and leave them.

"Where do you go, Rehsotis?" I hear the strained cry behind me as I approach the archway to the settlement. The sound of my given name pulls me to a stop. I turn and watch Brother Aelred stagger toward me.

"It is time for me to leave."

He drops to his knees at my feet and falls into a howling laughter. I do not expect it. It sounds unreal and unholy. He shakes his head and his laughter subsides, then he looks at me with a long-jawed slackened face. "You could not be gone too soon. For so long I have waited for you to leave. The others may not understand. Brother Cloaved certainly did not. But I have always known—you are an abomination. If you were away from here years ago, it would not have been early enough. With you away, it will be better for me. Better for us all."

I look down upon his clenched hands. His hatred opens his mind to me, his thoughts close the short distance between us, and I see the scene from long ago as clear as the full moon rising: Brother Aelred entering Brother Cloaved's chamber. Brother Aelred spewing words of hate to my dear, old friend. Brother Aelred brutalizing my gentle, dear, long-dead friend.

When I look into Brother Aelred's furious face, he sneers. "I nearly got rid of him then. The creature. He did not belong with us. When he touched the sheets of gold, or handed me a mortar filled with aquamarine, he revolted me. But I took care of that. I silenced him. How well I silenced him. But you… you are strong. I could not deal with you so easily. How long I have waited, and now at last the brotherhood shall be pure."

Within a heartbeat, I am upon him. I tear at him with a rage not felt before. The anger and hurt from years of regret and grief coalesce into that moment. I wrench his neck with my hands. It is an easy span. I tighten my grip. I do not yield. Without flinching, I watch Brother Aelred's eyes grow large. Beneath my tight thumbs and fingers, his pulse slows, slacks, stops. When his body collapses against my hips, I do not let go. His torso slumps to the stone path. Still, I do not let go.

In the distance, I hear the brothers finishing their prayers, their amber toned voices wrapping about the gentle pulse of the waves below. With little effort, I hoist the dead body of the creature responsible for wounding one of my dearest friends. His vile self will not remain with the brothers. In my fury it is easy to carry Brother Aelred's body to the kneeling stone, and I drop it over the far north ledge of the skellig, just beyond Brother Angus' grave. Beneath me, pearl-rimmed breakers pull him into their grip, and throw him again and again against unreachable stone ledges.

The brothers will wonder about the disappearance of us both. They may wonder, but they will now be safe from their own monster.

As for me, I dwell upon those parting words from Brother Angus—the prospect that Yargis is not dead and that he may have left for reasons about which I can only wonder. The array of reasons burns and flames for me like a beacon upon the horizon.

* * *

The Smallheaded make landfall during a moon-filled night. The entire skellig shifts beneath my feet when it happens—a sinking, a breach. From their sleek and shallow-hulled craft, the invaders take smaller boats and upon them make way into the shallow waters of the inlet at the skellig's calm east approach. I huddle in a breach of rock above their landing and bide my time.

The Smallheaded from the long ships snake their way up into the settlement and are greeted by a torch-lit line of quiet men, each holding an offering of bread, mead, and salted fish. Their red-cloaked leader declares the search for treasures will begin at dawn. With their bellies filled, and content with such an easy victory, the Smallheaded sleep deep and unperturbed, setting only a duo of the youngest upon night watch. The next day they search for a hidden chamber or vault within the dome-shaped chambers of the settlement, certain gold cups or other offerings from hopeful pilgrims waited somewhere. But they find nothing of riches.

When the moon goes dark several days after their arrival, I creep to where the small landing craft rest and the small team of drunken guards asleep. Nothing distinguishes the black wool felt sky from the smooth ink water. The liquid sea mirrors the dense net of stars, and I am contained within a sphere of glittering lights. I ease one of the leaf-shaped landing boats into the water. The outline of the skellig recedes, tethered to me only by the rippling wake of the boat that carries me, and I do not try to sense if I will ever return to the brothers. Instinct guides me toward the mainland, and the flash of the Smallheadeds' fire at the entrance of the monastery dims. Between the quiet strokes of my paddle, I hear only echoes of their singing and chanting.

With each surging stroke away from the Island of the Brothers, I feel an increasing sympathy for what the brothers face. My heart stirs tenderly for some of the brothers who took me into their midst and offered me shelter. In the depth of my grief, they provided a measure of comfort and quiet. Even grace. With my departure, I believe I protect not only myself, but the brothers for which I care. Upon leaving, I safeguard them. If these Smallheaded are, as I suspect, connected to Beowulf and his kind, they will want my life and the lives of any presenting sympathy for me. I push away any sense of abandoning them to an unearned fate at the hand of these marauders.

I glide through the night and into a morning sky clouded and curtained by low floating scarves of mist. My paddle dipping and lifting from the water creates a rhythm with my breath, and I float upon it undistracted for several days. When a blood moon rises, I curl up at the bottom of the Smallheaded's craft, hold my knees to my chest and bury my face in my arms. I drift into a blank and imageless sleep in which I want to rest for as long as possible. Then my slumber opens like the curtained entrance into a tent, and what promised to be an eternal night is fractured by a vivid dream. After ages of not encountering him in my dreamscape, he is here: Beowulf. When I try to dissolve away his image, to remove him from my near hibernation, he only gains in density and detail. This is not an uninvited page from my own book of memories.

He has sought me. He has found me.

"Leave me." I unfold into my full height to meet him eye to eye.

"Why? What brings you to me?"

It is now that I notice the wash of blood from his brow, the bright flowering of red across his chest and down both thighs.

"I am dying."

"Dying? It is not possible that you are dying now. Even the strongest of your kind could not live those many eras. The time when you brought death upon my family is ages past."

Beowulf's dark and hollow eyes widen.

"You must be between realms. What is it you last remember?" I do not feel sympathy, but I do want to hear his story.

"I battled the dragon. The creature your kind surely conjured. Perhaps you even conjured him. Yes, that would fit well with this story and my long age of reckoning. I battled the dragon, and now I have come to battle you, the creature who conjured it."

"Dragon? I conjured no such creature."

"I believe you lie. The dragon descended upon my holdings from many lands away. The look and fire of its eye burned with the same evil as your creatures. As I battled that possessed monster, I could hear in its wailing the language of your kind. It spat out Anathian. When it brought down its wrath full upon me, and I knew the wounds to be mortal, I called upon your kind and I saw the creature pause. It flinched. That was its one error. That hesitation gave me all I needed to drive my sword home to its heart. I may be about to walk into the darkness of death and nothingness, but your creation descended to its hell before."

"I assure you, I am not the creature you seek. I have had nothing to do with dragons or your other enemies."

"At first I didn't even know where the spirits were driving me." Beowulf continues to speak as if he does not hear me, as if he were looking through me. "But then I saw the long ships, and I felt the surge and bearing of the currents carrying them forth, and so I followed them. And now I find you. A creature like those I battled, so many years ago, in my youth."

"I am not 'like' those you battled in your youth. I am one of the same. You were nearly brought to your death by my brother Grendel and my mother Yenheth. And they were not creatures. They were my brother. My mother. You—you are their murderer."

"Brother and mother? Is this true?" Now his eyes focus upon mine.

"You say you are at your time of reckoning, you who killed my family. The spirits bring you here not because you think I created the dragon stronger than you. They brought you here for other reasons."

"I did not know until now there was another." Beowulf shakes his head and presses the palms of his hands to his temple where his once heavy plaits are unloosed, stringy and white.

"Until now? You did not know there was another?" I spit the words out as if they are poison. "You struck and killed without even bothering to find out the nature of your prey. Well, listen now and learn. I am of the Tribe of Anath. You should take more care with your words. Certainly you died long ago and your spirit has been driven to find me. That is the only explanation. That is why you are here in my dream. From wherever you were, until now, your spirit was driven here to me. You need to understand better what you did not comprehend in your youth. If you are not able to do so, please, leave my dream world." Revulsion fills me. I want his bloodied form to disappear.

"I have been brought here for reasons." Beowulf shudders, filled, perhaps with the same sort of loathing I feel for him.

"You must confront me. You are here to account for your past, do you not understand that? To ask for mercy for your actions."

I sense Beowulf blundering with his convictions, thoughts darting between self-doubt and guilt. If I push him beyond the edge of my dreamscape, he will be lost to the darkness, his unmoored spirit left to drift for eternity.

"Since the time when you battled my brother and murdered my

mother, what have you done? What have you realized?" He stares at me, eyes wide and mouth open, as I continue. "Are you here to ask for forgiveness? Do you even know why you are here?"

"Let me tell you what I witnessed." My own voice is certain as the pitch-dense hull of my boat. "You destroyed my brother and murdered my mother. You and your kind have torn apart my tribe, my family, and now, as you are about to pass into darkness, into forgetfulness, you are mute. Such is the hero of the Smallheaded. What would your tribesmen say about you now? What songs would they offer if they were to see you such as you are now?"

"I did not realize you were there."

"As if it would have mattered. What would you have done had you known of me? Turned against me next?"

"I do not know." He looks down at his hands clasped together at his waist. "I only know the torment I feel now."

In the moments of silence that follow, I realize that we begin to breathe in unison.

"I believe this—you are my confessor."

"Your confessor." I spear the dark with the words. "With what expectation? Do you expect absolution from me?"

"That must be it. As you tell me—I did not bid you. I was brought to you. I am not alive and am not dead. I cannot expect absolution. But perhaps I could ask of you some particle of resolution. I do not know what you believe, what myths and gods have directed your kind. But here I am. With you. I was brought— compelled—to find you." Beowulf looks at me and tears fill his eyes. "I ruled a kingdom. I watched as one faith overcame an ancient one, and not without some regret. I fought many battles but left behind no legacy of flesh and kin. After my time at the Hall of Hrothgar, I was beloved by my people. Yet I stand here now before you. I have heard your story. I must account for my actions against you. Believe me when I tell you—I regret what I did to your family."

"So you see clearly your defining moment. The one that resonates through the whole of your life and the one for which you will most be remembered." I take one step toward him but do not threaten him with raised fist or voice. "You destroyed my family. I hold your fate in my hand. Shall I abandon you here in this nether sphere—dead to one world, but not present to the next. I should have killed you in the cave, before you killed my mother. Even before you hurt my brother."

"When could you have done that?" He furrows his brow as he looks at me.

"First at the entrance of the hall when you and Grendel fought—I lurked there and would have had the advantage of surprise. I could have broken you in two and shattered your life, but I did not."

"You were afraid." Beowulf's eyes narrow. I expect him to sneer, but he does not. The words are spoken soft, almost in wonderment.

"I did not understand my power."

"You said you could have killed me another time."

"When you hunted down my mother Yenheth."

His eyes close and he whispers, *"Mother."*

"I was there, hardly an arm's reach away from you. Invisible to you. Again, you would have been taken by surprise, and with such ease. You did not realize, as you took my mother's life, our stories surrounded you. If you had only looked. The walls of our chambers were covered with pictures and charms, revelations and poetry the likes of which you could only guess. But you saw none of it. You were blind to the notion that some other could have similar worth, density, proportion… purpose. You only saw, as you call me, a creature."

"Why did you not make yourself known to me, why not take your advantage, as any warrior would to protect a brother, defend a mother? Does your tribe claim no familial honor?"

"Honor? Who are you to speak of honor? Because I did not strike? Regardless of cause—my fear, my essential loathing for your disregard for the core of life? You see it as a weakness, as a failure. But it is not." My throat tightens from the tincture of truth in those words. Even though we occupy my dream realm and not his, and I should have the advantage, I feel diminished.

Despite the impulse to flee this nether-room, I feel three immense forces: Yenheth, Yargis, and Brother Angus. At the periphery of my vision, I distinguish their outlines, intertwined if not interchangeable. The sovereigns of my family, my heart, my spirit—all so near and full of portent.

"Look at me." My words are clear as the chapel bell on the Island of the Brothers. "What do you see?"

Beowulf's image floats and shimmers like a fine sheet of gold leaf the brothers brushed upon a sheet of vellum.

"What do I see?" He stands wounded and gilded before me. He touches the edge of the boar-head shaped helmet he wears.

"What do you see before you?"

"I see—a creature."

"A woman."

"Not as intended. You are something unnatural."

"But we are a part of the same world. Agreed?"

"Yes."

"Then how can I be unnatural?"

"You are unknowable."

"That is not true. You chose not to know me. To know any of us. When you battled Grendel, and later my mother Yenheth, your actions were unnatural."

"I do not understand you."

But Beowulf does. He reveals this with the curving of his shoulders, the lowering of his head.

"We all—you and your warriors, my brother, mother, fellows— wanted to claim everything around us. We wanted to believe we were entitled to it all. And any other who so claimed, they became an enemy."

I say this more to myself than to the dream self of Beowulf.

"Your kind has taken the most, but you have lost at least as much as we have. Even more. We are each diminished, and that cannot be altered. My kind lost the bold beauty of hope and became more lost than ever before. The moment we stepped out of the garden, we recognized what made us different. And we feared each other. We let that fear determine our boundaries. And now it is very likely I am alone. Because of you and your kind, because of your greed fueled by your fear, no one else remains of my tribe."

Dark shadows of our shared dreamscape surround us and we drift into colors of flame and sea. We are quiet, and we bridge the silence with our breath and our gaze.

"I am filled with bitter contrition," Beowulf says at last.

Just then his clear image bursts open like a brittle seed pod and the fragmented vision begins to spread apart.

"Is this the beginning of redemption? Does that call to you? Is that what you seek? Is that what we are able to offer each other?" I ask his departing image.

"Can I not gain forgiveness without your mercy?" Blood begins to bubble from his mouth.

I am asking the same question of myself.

"I did not think so, until this moment." He continues, wheezing. "I did not believe I needed absolution from your kind for anything. I confessed my sins and offered my fully justified story. I never regarded my decisions with any regret."

"Then we differ greatly there. I regret much."

"And now, so do I." Beowulf gasps, his image now undistinguishable. "Do not regret any future decision. You have not finished your story. Our story."

"Our story?"

"Your story is a part of mine. The story is written on your body,and is carried in your soul. It weaves us together."

"And because you know my story you think you own it?" My words feel as thin as the dream.

"I must own my part of it." His words drift and swirl around me as if made of dust.

"Your part of it."

"And I have at last accounted for it. You shall do what you will. I cannot offer you more. This is the end of my story. My part in your story." And then, once more Beowulf the warrior appears whole before me and reaches out a hand as if to touch me.

I extend my right hand toward him. "Which causes you more pain? The words unsaid or the words not said well enough?"

Just as I am about to touch him, he shimmers and disappears without answering.

Next my dream fills with images of Grendel, Yenheth, Illisante, Brother Cloaved, and Brother Angus. They do not speak, and linger only a few moments. When Yargis appears, I try to hold him and ache to see him clearly for a moment longer. As his image fades, his eyes gleaming, he calls to me, "Oh, my heart's desire."

The full weight of the night engulfs me. I ebb into my body and the motion of the sea. The hull of the boat is slick with the sea's phosphorescent infusoria. I slip into the smooth water and float there until my own skin glows. In that moon-filled night, my flesh seems made of moonlight. I clamber back into the craft and curl at its center and fall back into sleep. This time without any dreams, without visitation.

I drift for weeks, dozens of moons. The current gains strength and the sea washes warmer. One red-rimmed morning, I awaken with a bone-deep sense of my bearings and discern the rough dark edge of land upon the horizon.

Before next nightfall, I make land and crawl upon the shore with a renewed sense of purpose and assurance. If Yargis be alive, I will find him. If others of the Tribe of Anath are near, I will rejoin them.

PART THREE

CONVENT

In a deep hillside den, hidden by dense grasses and graceful nut trees with leaves that sigh hushed melodies, I take shelter to better observe who lives in these surroundings and in what condition. The wild onion and sorrel I pull from along the riverbank tempers my indulgences in sweet-centered shellfish uncovered from the green mud of the backwater. The luxury of unframed time affords me silent healing and preparation, the recalibration of mind to heart.

I return to rhythms similar to those before I came to the brothers, of being adrift. I sense no other like myself in my dreams. No Smallheaded passes along the path marking the edge of the riverbank. For several seasons I languish in a deep, regenerative sleep.

Upon waking, I feel stronger and find spring surrounding me. The broom blooms vibrant yellow. Exposed cedar roots and trembling moss perfume softening mists. The hills angle blue shadows across deep gullies. Small creatures snuffle the edges of the season, and their grubbing hunger inhabits every moment. And in the midst of the surrounding world's increasing attentiveness, I do not find any echo of my Anathian tribe. Not even a murmur.

I wander first through a small spread of forest that rolls down to the riverbank; the river flows green and clouded between widespread banks. After my centuries living upon the rough and rocky sea-surrounded skellig, the rippling river and its mossy banks invite quiet contemplation. The river serves as a route and guide into an unfamiliar ease. An unkindness of ravens cluck smug, insistent warnings from their tall-pine roost.

Tentative, yet curious as hunger, I follow a deep and rutted road that meanders from the river toward another wide grove bordering a stream. In the quiet loaming, I pass the edge of a wide and flat marsh, then several neat and barren cultivated fields. At the edge of the fields stand the first of several rows of stout structures built of ragged yellow stone and even rectangles of sod. Timbers frame the remaining rooflines. Clutches of reeds and dense weaving vines choke roof beams and doorways. I stop, frozen in momentary apprehension in this village that could well be filled with Smallheaded. I hope to scavenge a trash pit or unattended storeroom for hard slices of rye tack or a round of mottled cheese—something prepared and not merely harvested or collected. My mouth waters, anticipating a few of the rich flavors I learned to appreciate during my time with the brothers.

Darkness pushes into every cranny. No lamplight. No quiet sigh of gathering and collective slumber. All is vacant. A vein without pulse. The only breath I detect is from small creatures—the nest makers and scavengers—emerging from their hidden tree-trunk roots and wall-beam crannies for their nocturnal gatherings. Overhead fly several silent-winged raptors, scanning with their keen eyes all the exposed and promising spaces for these vulnerable, tender-footed prey.

And yet, despite all evidence that the village is deserted, I do not venture forward for some time. I find a quarry that opens from a rocky culvert and take cover behind stacks of well-formed and finished stone to keep watch for any movement. It is then I notice how most of the village dwellings are fashioned from similar blocks.

As morning arrives, I steal into the village, now certain it is uninhabited. I wonder what devil or angel brings about such silence.

I walk to the first dwelling, crouch below an opening in the wall, and listen. Hearing nothing, I stand and peer inside. The sight pulls my stomach tight, and bile rises unbidden into my mouth. In the single room, a dozen Smallheaded bodies stretch out on pallets, side by side on the floor. A figure dressed in monk's robes sits folded stiff over the one table at the center of the room. The morning light falls upon the monk's left hand, which rests upon a plate. It looks as if all blood and fluid have been sucked from it, with nails long and yellow, knuckles and bone in mummified relief. A thick breeze brushes past my face at that moment, heavy with restless spirits and the anguish of ceaseless and frequent death. I bolt from the dwelling and find the same scene, with only a change in number or dress, upon throwing open one leather-hinged door after another. I flee the village, taking nothing.

* * *

For countless nights after I find the Village of Death, I dream-glide over the river, searching for some rippled thought to lead me to the living. After months, I am drawn toward the near howl of someone living. Smallheaded or Anathian, I cannot tell. Close to the dark, sparkling surface of the water I glide, faster and faster as I draw nearer to the sound. Finally, within the rubble of the stone quarry, I find the dreamer. She huddles in illness, near death. I sense her life drifting out of her reach. If she dies while I am there in her dream, it will bring me close to the brink of my own death. But I need to learn if she knows of my tribe. I need to discover if there are others somewhere nearby. Bone-twisting agony stabs at my joints as I rummage deeper into the geography of her dream state. What I enter is a horrific storm of red fire and lightning. A tidal pain pulls over her, and her thoughts offer nothing grounded enough for me to grasp or latch upon. I feel my very soul being sucked into the swirl of her suffering. It is imperative that I imagine the deep blue of my cloak, try with all of my effort to see myself whole again, and leave this place. I manage it, and just as I leave her mind, some other great disturbance erupts where her memory boils with her dream, and within it I decipher the voices and cries of Anathian. Pressing back into the thickest twisting of her torment, this time I stumble upon her dream self. She tears at her hair with knobbled hands and pulls at her mouth as if to twist from it an ancient root of truth.

When she sees me standing before her, she covers her head with her arms and rocks back and forth. "No. No. Leave me. Now." Her voice sounds like rubble being kicked before her along a dark path.

"I will not until you give me answers to my questions." I smell her fear.

She whispers, "No, no. You must leave."

"I will not harm you. Understand that. You have seen others like me? Were there others? Is there even one other? I believe you know. Please—help me."

The woman stops rocking and shakes her head. When she peers up at me, she looks like a creature caged. "It does not matter any longer. We are doomed."

"It does matter. It is of great importance. Tell me." I soften my tone and do not try to terrify her further. I even reach out to touch her shoulder as if it were a wing, to conjure comfort and ease upon her, and as the numbing effects of the charm spread like a web from her aching joint over the rest of her body, tears of relief stream down her cheeks.

"Yes. There was one. One like you, only darker skinned and taller. Many seasons ago he came upon us. Long before the fever. He showed us how to fashion stone into better wall."

I move to embrace the woman, for my heart is pounding with certainty that Yargis was among them.

She backs away from me. "Do not come closer to me! No. Leave. You have no place here."

"But are you certain he was alone? I need to know." At this I take a step to cross to her, clasp her shoulders in my hands, and lift her from the ground.

"I have never seen another such as you since then." She gasps and looks down at me. "You are only a dream. You cannot be real."

"Believe me. I am here and very real."

"Why did he leave you? Do you know why?"

"He hardly spoke to us. He only worked with us. Showed us what to do to build a stronger wall for a storehouse. A dwelling. And then he was gone. Please leave me. I know nothing, nothing more than that." Now she screams and I hear voices echo against the walls of her mind. I set the woman down gently, and she falls to her knees weeping. The pain of her body draws around her and pulls her into a pouch of death just as I move out of her dream.

* * *

I wander through more villages silenced by the recurring fever. I walk for months and encounter not another living soul. The bloom and color of spring fills the landscape, underscoring my solitude. In most villages, goats and swine, having broken free of their stalls or pens, wander in and around the huts and dwellings. Sometimes a set of fluttering rusty wings surprises me as a flock of hens bolts from a doorway. I find their eggs and add their richness to my next meal.

Eventually I do not even look inside huts or structures. The same sight always greets me: Smallheaded dead in various states of decay.

I roam south and east for a while longer. Then I come upon a divide in the path. One continues south. The other leads northwest, in the direction of the sea. To the south, I sense nothing more than a desperate emptiness. To the north, at least, awaits the sea, and I crave its salt-washed comfort and familiarity. I make my choice.

I come upon her just as I crest a hill. She rides on the back of an ox. A cloak of patch-worked red and green covers her, the colors heightened against the deep blue of the sea spreading out before us. Two large wide-woven baskets filled with wool bounce against each side of her beast. The sky is azure embellished with only a few full clouds. The still air enlarges the sea's surging breath below us. Above the rhythm of the waves, I hear her singing, in a voice as rich as Brother Cloaved's, and only a little higher. As a platter-shaped shadow of a cloud sweeps over both of us, she turns and looks at me. She does not stop singing and lifts an arm in a welcoming gesture. When I am closer, I see her eyes are blue as lapis lazuli and her cheeks freckled. I want to laugh. Truly laugh. Laughter is too long a stranger to me. But when the woman begins to laugh, I cannot help but join her.

* * *

With Abbess Carmelia, first there is laughter. We look at each other and laugh. Her laughter is not a gradual easing into full jubilation, but arrives as a full-trumpeted fanfare. Even before we speak to each other, we read each other's hearts with ease. She nods her head, points toward the hill lifting nearest the sea, and I follow her, laughing. She starts to sing a simple string song—one note sustained for several counts before sliding another radiant pearl onto the strand of the luminous timbre of her voice. Her song dashes away the images of the corpses in the strings of villages through which I journeyed. Without understanding the meaning of her words, I readily mimic the undulating syllables of her song:

> The sun, she is not silent.
> She fills my soul with warmth.
> She promises a golden season
> and here my heart is glad.
> She is the heart of wisdom
> giver of all life.
> Whenever I behold her
> I lift my heart to sing.
> And as I rest within her arms
> the world at last is blessed.

The brush of spring dapples the single-noted blue sky with blushing pink and buttery gold. A muffling density of cedar presses against the horizon. And then, such a breathing of red; inky dark-hearted blossoms turn and lift in chorus with the sea breeze, urging us on in our song, moving our steps forward. The blurred waves of red become distinguishable as fields of poppies, and once my eyes adjust to the bright red against blue, I see the convent nestled into the midst of the scarlet caps like a contented hen.

"There. Home." Abbess Carmelia repeats the words again and again until I take her meaning. She turns to me and waits until she is certain I understand. I nod and continue to walk beside her, and we pass together through the blue shade of the convent's limestone archway.

When the brothers had taken me in, I was not conscious and barely aware of their arms embracing me. I was at their mercy. This time it is my decision. I can turn and walk away from this settlement. But I do not. I look into the clear eyes of the heavily cloaked Smallheaded woman, and in my own tongue speak the most pleasing of all words in any language: "*Yes.*"

* * *

Another who calls herself Sister Agatha takes me to a small room—one of dozens of simple cells along the narrow corridor bordering the length of the Common Hall. She speaks the same language as the brothers and acts as interpreter between me and Abbess Carmelia during my first days at the convent. Her voice slides upon a velvet ground of amber as glowing as her eyes. At evening she comes to my door, offers a cup of mead and chunk of rusk. I welcome her to the low stool at the door. She peers out at me from beneath her hood.

"You know Abbess Carmelia is of noble birth?"

"No, I do not know this." The rusk is spicy as it crumbles against my tongue.

"Well, she is indeed. Such a story." Sister Agatha clucks her tongue and smooths her robe over her knees. "Her father expected her to marry a man named Aelthrun from a southern noble family. But before having met or married him, she gave birth to twin sons. Her father banished her, but her mother's family secreted her away. Or some said they believed the family of the twins' father did so. She did not remain with them…whichever family it was, I don't recall, and she was left to wander. She traveled by foot until she came to a desert place—the First Sacred Order of the Heart.

"And, oh, how taken was our dear sister with what she learned. She learned how to garden and how to grow our poppies. She learned all the songs we sing. The healing arts. How to pray and how to read dreams. She lived with them for many years, and then she experienced her vision."

Sister Agatha shakes her head and turns an earnest face to me. "It was what changed her. It came at first to her soft and gentle, and when she refused to believe it was a gift that needed to be brought to reality, the vision became increasingly vivid, nearly searing as it tore into her dreams and her waking thoughts. It would rattle her from slumber or her meditation and leave her weeping. In her vision she was shown by Our Blessed Mother to walk a long path returning north. And she did not want to go. Then Our Blessed Mother showed her building the convent not far from her father's land. And she did not want to build. Our Blessed Mother showed her leading a group of women and others who wanted to be closer to the divine. But she did not want to lead."

"What changed her heart?"

"Every Abbess Carmelia dreamed about our fields, our tables, the communal fire in the Common Hall, and even more—our faces, down to the color and shape of my eyes or even Sister Clarice's manner of jutting her chin in and out. Everything you see here now. All of us. In such detail she will tell you could even smell the lamps burning in the chapel. And yet some of us were not even born. Can you imagine that? No other life seemed possible. It was demanded of her. She demanded it of her."

"She?"

"Our Blessed Mother. She. She is God."

* * *

Abbess Carmelia calls it the Warring Age. Her convent is a small clutch of peace within decades of death and war. When she began receiving "her pilgrims," there were soon some fifty women drawn to her gate. With each new moon, others arrive to live in the convent with her, and the numbers of pilgrims and seekers increase. Sometimes a pilgrim or two will leave, returning to her kin or to set out on her own journey to their Jerusalem. The convent functions best with a company of nearly one hundred.

The land demanded a harsh and proscribed life for the brothers. But here with the sisters, the seasons and earth are temperate and rich. The growing time spans several months and the generous nature of the soil supports appetites for rich flavor. Soon I help in the gardens where we grow many of the same root crops tended by the brothers, especially the turnips and parsnips able to survive anywhere; here those same varieties thrive in heavier quantities. Grunting, we pull free from the earth their ample hearts, some snowy as a wolf moon, others garnet as a lamb's liver. Elegant vines heavy with jewels of proud aubergine and tender spring peas sway above rows of skirted stout cabbages and plummy fennel. Dense hedges of herbs such as rosemary, sage, and lavender lean into each other like sentries around each garden. The pathways grow thick with thyme. Clumps of garlic, chives, and mint spread with green abandon against arbors and benches.

Added into the abundance of the gardens are the nearby woodlands' tender ferns, sedges, and morel mushrooms, which become fleeting savory notes in soups and stews prepared in the kitchen. Shared meals are celebrations of flavor, introduced and carried forward by song.

After evensong, dinner often occupies most of the night, with Abbess Carmelia carrying the pitcher brimming with wine she makes each year using grapes gathered from the arbors encircling her hut.

As she pours the red wonder into each cup, she throws back her head in laughter. "Now, this is how to worship our Blessed Mother." Then she fills her own goblet and asks for another song.

* * *

My cell near the southern end of the Common Hall opens upon a deep cloister of braided willow that wraps around the second floor of the building. The verdant air tastes salty from the sea breezes. Here the sisters stroll in either solitary thought or in pairs or trios of companionable conversation. I lean against a limbed arch and watch the sea blend blue into an expansive sky. As I warm myself in the early spring sunshine, Abbess Carmelia works in her vineyard. She talks to the vines as she examines their leaves reaching out from the stem like green hands, kneels to clear thatch and weeds from around their thick trunks.

She looks up to see me watching her. "Come, come join me."

Her voice pulls me from my somnolence and to her side. "Here, help me trim." She hands me a triangle of flint polished smooth and honed at the edges, and shows me how to make the vines lean of leaf with gentle turns of the wrist. "With fewer leaves, the fruit will be able to feel more sun and stretch full with joy. And then, when we come to the time of veraison, I will begin to taste the blushing fruit, and mark my word, I will be able to predict the flavor of the wine from the bite of the juice."

She taps my arm with her flint and nods. Above us a jay skims and dips, teasing her for attention.

"There will be plenty for you, too." She scolds the bird. "Some complain that the birds destroy the orchards. I believe that if we attend the orchard well, it offers enough fruit for all of us. Don't you agree? I planted several rows with them and for them. And then we agreed that they leave the rest for us."

"And what about the poppies?" I turn toward the hillside to the north where the poppies have just burst open. Their red tinges the air just above their heads with quivering ribbons of persimmon.

"Our poppies. Treasures for us, indeed." Abbess Carmelia takes my arm and we begin to walk toward the inner green of the convent. "Long ago, I brought a pocketful of poppy seed pods with me from the east. I spread those seeds along the path leading to our gate. There were only a dozen or so of us sisters gathered together at the time. Think upon that. In the seasons that followed, the poppies thrived and spread. I would harvest more of the seeds and scatter them over the hillcrests and fields around us. They are happy, are they not? Now they fill the fields with their beauty, and no one remembers a time when they did not grow here. And as with the poppies, there are many more of us here caring for each other and Our Blessed Mother."

The brilliant poppy blooms do not last long. Just as their vibrant color curls and drops away, Abbess Carmelia leads us into their midst. With our thumbnails we split open hundreds of pods and scrape their milky bitter sap into curved vials strung upon leather cords tied about our waists. In the evening, the day's collection is stirred and simmered into tar-colored clay and rolled into small balls. Still more dark-hearted pods are gathered into satchels to dry and grind for tea. At the infirmary, those giving birth or those welcoming death will be ministered to by the sisters who have cultivated their gifts of healing. They know which proportion of the poppy's magic results in a painless birthing, how much pressed against a fevered tongue will ease a pain-curled sister to a gentle rest, or help her drift into her passing, smiling, sometimes even singing. By the time we finish our harvest, and the winds clean the last lingering petal from the furred and dusty green leaves, it is early summer.

I wear the soft and gentle folds of linen, over which I wrap an ample tunic covered with deep pockets. I dress the same as all of the sisters. We fill our pockets with our particular treasures. In mine I keep all manner of things—a Latin primer, a handful of toasted nuts, a honed shell with which to cut flower stems, a fire stone and striker, graceful wave-shaped pieces of driftwood, and a gathering of lavender.

When we work in the fields, orchards, or vineyards, the prevailing breeze from the cove twists and pulls at our voluminous gowns, and we appear like a flock of graceful sea birds. No one calls me Other. They call me Sister Rehsotis.

* * *

The convent wall encircles seven swathes of high ground. Within its limestone embrace rests the one Common Hall that houses all of us; each of us has our own small cell, containing a sleeping pallet, a squat chair, and a trunk made of willow and linen for our belongings. Next to the door are three hooks for cloaks and tunics. The long two-storied dormitory connects to the common kitchen and dining hall by a covered passageway. We eat in the same large room in which we cook. Seven firepits with clay ovens hunker like sea turtles down the center of the hall. All sisters and able-bodied pilgrims share a rotation of meal duties. Bread is baked each morning from a simple mix of flour, water, and beer. Into the largest pot at the center daily gatherings from the garden are set to a slow, fragrant, and constant stewing. Along the walls we hang braids of garlic and onions, and wreaths of peppers and herbs. When it rains, the earth around us exudes a dense, comforting perfume of mint and bay.

Across the common gardens from the dormitory stands the round-roofed structure Abbess Carmelia calls the Hall of Learning. Here the sisters teach pilgrims to read from the sizable library of scrolls collected during Abbess Carmelia's several trips to the East, augmented and enlarged with codex contributed by the most affluent visitors to the convent, and volumes transcribed by the sisters dedicated to scrivening. Many of the youngest daughters of noble families arrive with at least a few books in their tapestry satchels. Most do not know how to read upon arrival, but in short time, with one of the sisters at a pilgrim's side whispering encouragement against their bended heads, long hair braided down their patient backs, that changes. The world opens to them within their hands, and they move through it with each page turned. Long tables occupy the center of the hall where several sisters spend their days transcribing copies of the volumes. The most experienced group is entrusted with embellishment and artwork for the manuscripts. When pause is taken from their work, they gather to talk and read aloud to each other.

Through a wide arch in the Hall of Learning wall facing the rising sun we approach the Gathering Hall. Here at morning, midday, and after evening meal, the sisters sing communal prayers to their Blessed Mother. We move to the sung lines while kneeling upon tapestry cushions stuffed with rosemary and lavender, their fragrance adding their own melody. At each gathering, Abbess Carmelia tells a story or recites a poem, sometimes something familiar, or something improvised. A sister or a pilgrim dances to the front of the hall and sways within the pool of light falling from the cross-shaped lantern hanging above, and offers one of her own stories. A quartet of the younger women jumps up and pantomimes her story. Always there is song. Our evening gatherings do not end until well after midnight. The thickening shadows are dispersed by our adding the amber light of the lanterns and building higher the fire in the pit at the back of the hall.

The Temple of Healing stands apart from the two joined halls. The structure is long and thatch-roofed, and several wide openings in the limestone walls let in air and light but are angled to keep out wind or rain. Tapestries hang over cords drawn tight from one wall to another and divide the space as needed into smaller spaces.

"At times, those in need of healing, those making their final passage, or visitors bringing forth babes needing to feel safe within a quiet room." Abbess Carmelia caresses the head of a sleeping girl. "And the space must be beautiful. Beauty is its own healing power, so Our Blessed Mother has told me."

When again the recurring fever sweeps with insatiate greed from one village to another, word of the healing powers offered at the convent draws seekers of a cure daily to our gate. We spread pallets beneath awnings fashioned from tapestries from the eaves of the Temple of Healing. After mothers bring forth their babes, often they stay with us until their offspring toddle on robust legs; the mothers learn from the tales of the sick and dying around them that their villages fall silent behind the curtain of certain death from the recurring fever. The sisters do not ask, but sufferers insist they accept tokens of gratitude: heavy gold coins, soft bundles of longhaired fleece, amphora of scented oils.

The only other structure within the circular wall of our convent is the hive-shaped Tapestry Hall. It stands like an eye in the center of the forehead of the convent, just north of the Temple of Healing. Here we spin and twist the wool and flax, stretch the strands upon the frames that stand like ribs at the center of the large room. The sisters weave the tapestries in shades of milk and earth, then stitch and embroider nearly life-sized depictions of images from books treasured in the Hall of Learning. In the drying shed, the sisters crush plants and shells, and bend over receipts written by Abbess Carmelia in her leaning script from formulas learned when she was in the East. The brilliant hues from these dyed threads and strands come to life with the sisters' agile skills. Their needles dance over and under the warp threads, interlacing with and concealing the muted background.

Each sister wears a cord around her neck from which hangs a bronze pendant pressed with a map of the convent. The edge of the amulet is crenelated to suggest the limestone wall, with a gap in the pattern at the bottom representing the gateway. At the top, the round shape of the Tapestry Hall; beneath it, two thick rectangles representing the Temple of Healing and the Gathering Hall. Below them, like a disarming smile upon a face, the Common Hall yoked together to the Hall of Learning. This symbol is engraved or carved throughout the convent—into the wall at the front of the Gathering Hall, into wooden door-arches, ceiling capitals, or window lintels. In each and every corner of a tapestry, the symbol is embroidered in gold-twisted thread, and it is scribed upon every leather cover of a book in the Hall of Learning.

When a pilgrim or seeker approaches the convent, the sister on watch alerts us all by striking a string of clear and hollow tones from the gateway chimes. The shimmering notes rise above the constant call of sea wind. The sister assigned to greet new arrivals scurries to open the carved wooden entrance gate. Before permitting the single traveler or the pilgrim party admission, the sister asks three questions: "What brings you to our gate? What do you hope to find within our midst? What do you hope to create while in our heart?" It amuses me to think I have never been asked these questions.

The answers vary. It is not a test. The answers simply clarify for the sisters what is hoped of them, and what they can hope of the visitor. The answers tell much of what is found in the heart and soul of the new pilgrim, the exile, or the fugitive.

All of Smallheaded women arriving at the convent are welcomed, and most are of noble birth. Their numbers increase as word spreads of the easily used, certain power of pessaries and abortifacients carefully formulated by the sisters following Sister Carmelia's instructions. Depending upon the woman's age and stature, if the womb has quickened or fallen suddenly still, she will receive an ideal blend of juices from savin, rue, elleboros, calamint, aristolochia, and mugwort, kneaded with myrhh to be eased into the body or warmed in wine as an elixir. Even more, the promise of a pain-free birth with a potion of poppies is irresistible. The women gathered at the birthing bed always share prayers and tears, and they are accompanied with either relieved laughter—or stunned silence as grief holds its breath before shattering their hearts with its fists. The babe—whether flush with first breath or purple with defeat, roundedly whole or limply collapsed, and even sometimes having been disassembled into its parts to gain exit—is received the same: rubbed fragrant and warm with lavender oil, swaddled in a cloud of wool, and nestled against the bosom of the exhausted, waiting mother.

"These women know their selves best. One may be locked in a

cruel marriage. Another wants to leave the bondage of offering her body in exchange for shelter. Yet another is too young or too old. With a simple tincture or formula, she can retain agency over her life. I am her servant and provide what is needed to urge her terms or to expel an unwanted issue," Sister Carmelia explains. "Others may try to keep the wisdom of the plants from us. Not here. Here we believe a woman should be able to say yea or ne."

Some of the women do not want to return to their homes, even if they have the privilege of landed rank. The young mothers relish the work at the convent, the shared responsibilities. The rhythm of daily living, despite its demands, is lighter than what most know in their homes. The infants come increasingly under my care, and I gradually assume the role of nurse-mother. The softened hearts of new mothers accept me with ease.

"You are so strong and vigorous," a mother tells me as she rests her swaddled child into my arms. The babe's face turns and roots against my shoulder.

"Your babe will be well and thrive here in safety."

The mother closes her eyes and drifts into welcome sleep upon hearing my words.

The rhythm of my days is regulated by taking the infants to their mothers for nursing, whether they are at the Hall of Learning, in the gardens, or at some other task within the convent, and then I gather them back to either fall asleep curled safe within my arms or slung at my hip, or to crawl and play upon me, twisting my hair or toying with my long fingers. At night the infants sleep with me, nuzzled against my chest, legs, and back. When there are several, Abbess Carmelia brings extra pallets into my chamber to make us all more comfortable.

Abbess Carmelia cloisters herself in the hut with her visions, her diet of brown bread, goat milk, and poppy tea. Her visions make furious her quill. She scratches ink into the vellum, the nib of her pen hardly keeping pace with her recollections.

"I wish there were a way to write more than one thought at a time. If I were not limited to the linear line of words through which to transfer these stories from Our Blessed Mother, my time would be better spent." She shakes her head and blows the sand from the page to set the ink. She embellishes her words with charcoal and dyes. Her fingers are perpetually stained black, red, and orange. No color satisfies her. She tries again and again, and mixes blue, red, and yellow hues in various combinations trying to replicate what the drugged visions bring to her.

Her brown eyes glistening, she clutches my sleeve as I help her to her chamber after evening meal. "Our Blessed Mother told me I must not use color. No color. None at all. Only black upon the white page, that is what She said." Abbess Carmelia winces as if in pain. "She told me that if I render the vision well enough, the color will reveal itself to those who look upon the page."

* * *

For a long stretch of years, I do not travel through dreams into the night lives of the sisters. My bed is soft. I enjoy the love of the infants and permit their dreams to enter mine. That is a gift of all creatures' babes. Their pure spirits and the bare simplicity of their need for touch, love, safety, and food means they readily offer the wondrous turnings of their minds to any able and willing to experience them. Here I find a core of gentleness in the Smallheaded race. I learn how different they can be and that within their kind, there are tribes not driven to cause harm. My sympathy for these babes so moves me and softens my heart that my breasts fill with milk and I am able to suckle them.

* * *

It is the coldest and longest night of the winter when a sled pulled by a team of white horses arrives. Two fur-cloaked squires climb down from their seat, faces ashen and lips translucent blue from the cold. They help two women climb out from beneath dozens of thick robes. Both are draped in finely woven gowns of gleaming white.

"We are of the House of Galambos." One of the women speaks with a voice that breaks like tree limbs in a storm. "A noble house. I am her grandmother. Her grandfather's land and holdings are vast, but her father's heart is tight and ruined as an old wine skin. I fear I have waited too long, for my granddaughter already labors."

The young woman cries out and reaches for her grandmother who does not seem to hear.

"I will not forsake my own blood," the grandmother says. "I ask that you release my granddaughter from the pain of childbirth. She is too young. Too small. I fear for her life."

She gestures toward the sled. "We bring you gifts. Within these layers of fine fleeces you will find numerous treasures —boxes of powders for ink, folios of gold leaf, reams of parchment from distant lands. There are also sacks of grain, urns of dark honey, and colorful bags of spices."

"An abundance of riches, certainly," says Abbess Carmelia. "But those are not necessary." She comforts the old woman with affirmations and leads her to the common fire. Sister Agatha and I lift the laboring young mother onto a sling and carry her into the Hall of Healing. She does not open her eyes or say a word.

Later I come upon the noblewoman in the Hall of Learning bent over a thick Testament. "Even as they took her to the marriage bed, I knew in my heart it was wrong. She was not ready." The woman rests her head upon her arms and sobs. "My heart beats dark. She was always so full of light and music. The light of her soul has gone out. I am in fear of losing her."

Her fear proves true. The baby cries out for the first time just as her mother cries out for her last. The old woman weeps for the death and the birth. Abbess Carmelia, and I look down upon an infant ill-formed for this world. Where arms and legs should be are spoon-shaped flaps of flesh better suited to paddle water than stand upon the earth. Without speaking, Abbess Carmelia washes and swaddles the child, and places her in my arms.

"She needs you more than any of the others." With one look, I know she is not only entrusting her to me, but making her my own.

The grandmother will not touch the child. She leaves at dawn, and we never see her again.

The babe we call Galambos is a gift. My time with her carries me forward and deep into remembrances and dreams of Illisante. I wonder if the spirit that resided in one made her way to me and now resides within this helpless Smallheaded.

Galambos grows slowly. Sister Agatha weaves and embroiders a quilted sling in which I carry Galambos. She curls within it soft and full of contentment. It is easy for me to move her from around my waist, to the small of my back, my side or chest, depending upon whether I bend to pick finger-long beans in the garden, press into kneading dark dough, or pull red threads across a loom. I fix her near my shoulder to offer her easy access to my ear, her soft paddle-shaped hands gentling my neck and face. Often, I bend with the strap crossing my shoulder blades so the sling falls cradling Galambos near the ground, swaying and singing her favorite words in repeated and countless variations: *pomme, embrasser, cerise, enfant, Rehsotis.*

My name is lyric, verse, refrain. When I gather driftwood and other gifts from the sea, I set her down upon the shore where she pulls and pushes herself toward the waves. She lets the sea roll and rock her in its shore fingers. I watch over her, vigilant for a chin-led toss of her head and low guttural one-note call beckoning me to take her back into my arms and secure her against my body.

At the beach we always play the Sea Game. I take up a handful of sand and shells to spread over a woven mat next to where we rest. I place portions of soft bread I rolled into balls upon her tongue. She smiles and lets each rest there until it melts against her tongue. Then she swallows and scans the spread of sand and shells. I track the motion of her blue eyes and hold a cup of poppy and cardamom tea to her lips.

When her eyes fix upon a spot, I lift each shell and pebble within the circle of that focus until she trills her approval. I pocket the treasure and add it to her collection in my room that we now share.

The sea treasures fill our windowsill and circle around the edge of the floor of our room three times when Galambos slips away from life during her silent sleep in the deepest blue of a summer night. I gather the stones and shells into my sleeve and take them to the shore to toss them one at a time back into the sea. All but one—one rosy shell shaped like her ear by which to remember her short life.

* * *

Abbess Carmelia, Sisters Agatha, Magdalene, Judith, and I make our way back to the convent carrying baskets round-topped-full of poppy pods. We pause when we sight a flock of yellow-billed and sail-winged storks. They glide low above our heads toward the dense line of trees where clusters of their wagon-sized nests rest in the highest limbs. We laugh in admiration of the storks' dangling-legged and cross-shaped grace, and track their line of flight with our collective gaze to an indigo and magenta robed form just as it emerges from the forest.

Abbess Carmelia gasps, brings a long-fingered hand to rest upon her heart. "Can it be?"

"Who, Abbess? Who is it?" We narrow our eyes to focus on the form approaching.

"He moves like one of the storks." We laugh at Sister Agatha's joke.

Abbess Carmelia shakes her head and repeats softly, "Can it be? Can it be?" as the figure steadily makes his way to us.

He is tall for a Smallheaded man, nearly as tall as I. His eyes are not the light and ice blue of so many others, but flash dark, nearly black, and are the first thing noticed as he draws within ten paces of us. He pulls down the hood of his cloak and smiles, his lips full and teeth white and even as milk beans in their pod.

"It is you. Certainly I have found you, Carmelia." Like music her name flows through those lips, and the distance between them collapses, and all of us around them are gathered into a wind-muffled silence. It is as if we disappear.

"Avenar. How far you have come." It is a declaration and not a question.

"Quite far. And it would have been farther, if need be."

They stand facing each other for a few moments, and then she turns to us. "This is Avenar of Aleppo. We met in the desert when we were students of the Order."

Sisters Agatha, Magdalene, Judith, and I look at one and another and then at Abbess Carmelia. I recognize the expression on her face—I had found it reflected in Yargis' eyes when I looked upon him. And here, without apology or hesitancy, this man named Avenar gazes upon Abbess Carmelia with the same unchecked adoration.

"Please greet my dear brother of spirit and heart. From so long ago."

"Not that long ago." Avenar of Aleppo shakes his head.

"It seems so long ago. And so far away. From the desert of our pilgrimage, which brought us together, to this place of gathering."

Abbess Carmelia sweeps her arms out as if to encompass all of us standing there and the convent rising behind us.

With vigorous and warm embraces, Avenar of Aleppo greets each of us, repeating our names as if we are much missed and beloved sisters. And if Sister Margaret's truncated limbs, Sister Magdalene's ethereal beauty, Sister Judith's white and vacant eyes, or my altogether unusual appearance gives him cause to shrink away in alarm, he does not reveal it. He appraises each of us with the full intensity of his black eyes, and if there is anything other than joy in his heart, I do not sense it.

"Come. You must be tired. You will stay with us for a good long while. There is a north-facing room with a view of the sea waiting for you. And tonight we shall feast."

Swirled within the vibrant drape of his cloaks that deepen the colors of her eyes and his lips, they move away from us toward the convent. Abbess Carmelia takes Avenar's arm. As they walk before us the full spread of their robes entwine around them until it seems they are of one body, their two heads leaning close together.

We prepare for the greatest feast ever held at the convent. Dark honey sweetens the barley meal. We blend butter with coriander and dill for fresh loaves of bread. The wild boar—trapped in the forest and herded to a pen by Sister Margaret where she indulged him and made him slothful on berries and daily leftovers—is slaughtered. We reduce his blood into a dense red soup with cabbage and porrettes. We season and bake his head with garlic and wine. The tender-most portion of his loin is roasted with turnips and wrapped in sage. There are cooked eggs and chard tossed with salt, violets, and primroses. The fish stews to tender flakes with yellow beans in thick cream. Platters of golden melons and cheese are set all about our tables in the dining hall. As usual, Abbess Carmelia pours the mead and wine, and sings her thanks, cheeks flushed, eyes glittering. Between her and Avenar runs a current of heat and light so intense, some of the sisters need to look away and catch their breath.

After the first savory bites of the feast, Avenar takes from the satchel a psaltery made of mulberry, willow, and pear wood. Leather covers the sound board, and it is scribed with the same pattern embellishing the satchel. The pattern is repeated in white bone inlaid along the side of the stringed instrument. My own breath catches in my throat when he settles it in his lap and strums. His music echoes of the melodies I played on my instruments.

As he performs, he looks at each of us in turn, unhurried, and alters the theme for each of us; the rhythms and motifs he chooses match our personalities with beatific accuracy. When he looks at me, the tune turns luminous and sad. For the first time in a very long while, there is a fragrance to the music, a color and taste. When I was with the brothers, I could relish and join in the chants; here with the sisters I often see colors in the midst of their sung prayers. But here again, as when I was young and with my tribe, the other textures of music come to me. It is intoxicating, and as I look into Avenar's eyes, I taste pomegranate, inhale oleander, and view all through a transparent sheath of yellow. I believe all will be well as long as he is here with us, making music for us.

He turns to Abbess Carmelia sitting near his right. The music fills the room with such penetrating ardor; I cannot bear it any longer and slip away. Stars fill the night sky. Scarlet and emerald lights gush through the black canopy, spiral and stream away from each other. I stand outside watching the dancing stars and feel as if I were drunk on Abbess Carmelia's poppy tea. I retreat to my room, where I lie awake for a long time. The strummed paradise of Avenar's music drifts to me and mingles with a lark's yearning serenade in the early gray of dawn. At last I sleep and dream of Yargis, dream that he, our daughter Illisante, and I are together on an island, salty with joy and tender with belonging.

* * *

"Tell me, Sister Rehsotis, what must I tell Carmelia to convince her to join with me?" Avenar walks toward me as I tend the garden in a dew-cooled morning. He has been with us long enough that no one expects him to leave.

His choice of words makes me smile, and he coughs and waves a hand before his face, frustrated by the language he speaks with certainty but without the poetry of his mother tongue. "I want her to bring her work and the sisters of the convent, to be with me and the brothers of my monastery. I believe we can do much more together than apart."

I am silent, recalling how the residual light and sympathetic vibrations created by the two of them during many of these recent days and nights tear open and disrupt my own meditations and dreams. Their passion instills the very air with lingering images of the two of them together—her lips against his throat; his hands caressing the small of her back, the arch of a foot; her tongue sweeping the length of his thigh; his hip straining against her navel; her hair falling across his groin; his mouth savoring her breasts. Even during the daylight, images of their coupling open and close like a breathing tabernacle in my mind.

"The work of the convent is important here. There is no other such sanctuary for many miles. To whom would these women, these children, and the frail elderly turn?" I continue pulling errant sedges and grass from around the squash vines. Avenar kneels next to me and helps. His sunned skin is nearly as dark as mine and veins like a map of the world cross the backs of his hands.

"Perhaps one of the sisters could continue her work. Consider Sister Agatha. She is wise and kind, well instructed in the teachings of the Order. Or Sister Margaret. She seems to fear nothing, receives the respect and humor of all around her." Hope and yearning throttle his cider voice.

"I cannot remain much longer. My sanctuary is very near a common way for those on crusade or pilgrimage. We are often at risk. Those from the far reaches of the East come down upon us with increased frequency and violence. They seek our conversion. I have already persuaded two other convents and monasteries to regroup with us to increase our strength. I need to be there. I am their abbot. But I cannot bear to leave…"

I reach out and touch his wrist. "Then do not leave. If you were to leave, it would cause her unbearable grief. I do not sense that her heart will let her leave. She is bound to her vision, the one she experienced while at the Order. Certainly you know that?" I look into his dark eyes and see more torment.

"Did you know that I know how to make instruments such as the one you have?"

He wrinkles his brow. "I did not know, but I am not surprised. I sensed your singing heart the first night I was with all of you."

"I mention this because it is relevant. I do so long to again fashion such instruments for music."

"Then you should."

"I do not know if I could still make them as they should be. It demands more than a skill working wood to find the earnest tone. I think my heart aches too much for what is not here with me. I feel more content here with Abbess Carmelia and the sisters than I have for a very long time, but I too am separated from my people, from where I could find my heart's ease."

"If you were to press Abbess Carmelia into leaving this place, she will not have her heart's ease."

"Do I not bring her heart to ease?"

"The two of you are each other's beloved. But you know as well as I do—you have just alluded to it—not only do you wish to drive out those such as my tribe from every space, but any with a different code or variant appearance. We are vulnerable to those with the swiftest ships, greatest numbers, and strongest greed—that is cause for fear and strife among you. Only the rarest of your kind seem capable of setting aside differences. Only the most blessed seem capable of the sort of compassion Abbess Carmelia and you offer. Your beloved has created an island of dreams and safety here on this high hill at the edge of the sea. You tell me you are at the same work elsewhere. How can either of you abandon that to your passion for each other? Such young passion. And how can either of you abandon each other. Do you truly think you can do anything that will stem the tide of Smallheaded destruction?"

As I speak, Avenar pulls a clutch of sweetgrass from the earth, and twists and works it into a ball of green ooze. Tears streak his broad and smooth cheeks. As I speak, he stares at the lintel of the gateway to the convent engraved with its symbol. Finished with my words, I am silent at his side. At last, he draws in his breath and looks at me, then takes my soil-covered hands and presses each palm against his lips.

"Stories of beings such as yourself were told at the Order when Carmelia and I were taking instruction there." Avenar gently lets go of my hands.

"She never mentioned that to me. But it explains why my appearance never seemed to alarm her."

"Why would your appearance alarm anyone?" Avenar strikes a

mock serious tone with a momentary return of his humor. "I speak the truth. We were told of a grand and great race who could travel into the dreams of others as easily as their own, who were gifted in the ways of music and magic, and who, although taller and stronger than others, were unwilling to take advantage of such attributes. But I think Carmelia's lack of alarm when coming upon you had more to do with her own natural geniality than any foreknowledge. Her affection for all is entirely disarming and sincere."

"With her I have come to know an affection never expected from one of your kind. I did not even feel such welcome or understanding with the brothers far north."

"The brothers far north?" Although we speak of many things, I have shared little about my own life. "Years ago, at my sanctuary, Brother Gerald spent several seasons with us. Gentle soul. Spoke little. I recall him saying that he spent years in the company of one such as you. You seem much like the person he described."

"I suspect I am the she about whom you were told. Brother Gerald did reside at the monastery while I was there."

The garden has become cool in the gloaming, and we rise to walk toward the vineyard. Our sudden movement startles a gray shrike from her perch. Avenar tucks my hand under his arm. The sea wind quiets for a moment, and we are caught by the music of the waves and the scent of the grapes hanging in heavy, dusty magenta clusters.

"What of her dreams, Sister Rehsotis? What can you tell me of her dreams?"

"I rarely find my way into them, Avenar of Aleppo. Once or twice I have come upon them as we sleep. But those center upon the fields, the work of the convent and the sisters. I have not encountered your shadow here, but that means little."

I know this is not what he wants to hear, but I will not lie to him. "Sometimes, a dreamer is strong enough to keep closed the most precious and vulnerable images of her life. Some dreams, when too real, can cause lingering pain and longing. Even while awake, the recollection makes daily living unbearable. Abbess Carmelia would be such a stoic dreamer. She could well have wanted you in her dreams each night, but if she allowed it, she would be claimed by such an obsession, and would want to be dreaming always of you."

Again tears fill Avenar's eyes. From the far end of the vineyard, we hear Abbess Carmelia's voice in song. Without another word, I embrace the heartsick abbot, he turns from me, and walks toward the voice of his love. As he moves deeper into the rows of the spreading and reaching vines, I lose sight of even the top of his dark head.

It is not difficult to imagine what the two of them share in the vineyard that afternoon. When we gather for dinner, Avenar is dressed in the robes and cloaks he wore when he first arrived at the convent. He and Abbess Carmelia are not as quick with laughter as before. Their sadness and resignation are palpable.

Sister Margaret runs into the dining hall, calling out, "Come quickly. All of you. Outside, the heavens again weep."

We stream out of the dining hall and look up into the dark sky.

Above us the stars indeed are falling like glittering tears. Avenar of Aleppo leaves the convent before dawn.

* * *

The ill and the seekers continue to arrive at the convent defeated by despair and in good time depart restored by hope. Some bring missives from Avenar of Aleppo. After his visit and departure, Abbess Carmelia's trust in me deepens, and she shares the contents of these letters with me. In them he continues to plead with her to move with the sisters to his sanctuary. His loneliness for her drives the rhythm of his words. The letters also reveal his observations and understanding of the increasing strength of the bishop of the region. He writes of how impressed he is with the bishop's view of linking the efforts of many convents and monasteries, and that by working under the rubric of one unified vision of their christ, their future will be enriched and secured.

Abbess Carmelia folds a letter after reading it and tucks it into a leather satchel that hangs at the window above her bed. "I miss him, but he must understand our efforts are needed here. And I do not sympathize as he does with the church counsel or the bishop's desires. Instead, I am suspicious of such desires. I am suspicious of anyone capable of an influence so strong that it is altering Avenar's tone."

She caresses the satchel as if it were Avenar's shoulder. "Such gentle and loving words. So abundant and sincere. But now, more often, he sends biting passages motivated not by the desperation of an aching heart, but something more selfish."

After receiving these shaming and cutting assertions, Abbess Carmelia goes alone into the forest. She always returns, sometimes as the mourning doves oboe the dusk, sometimes at the next full moon, and takes up with her work and arts as though her heart were not breaking.

Their letters, still seasoned with the underpinnings of their passion for each other, become laden with passages delineating their diverging views of the Christ and the purpose of their own work. The words are strident, political, and argumentative. She insists upon a church where each community can articulate their own purposes and works. He insists, with a tone more often threatening than beseeching, upon a set of common principles without room for "frivolous energies."

When Abbess Carmelia shares the last letter with me, she spits out the words.

"My work here and how I go about it is not 'frivolous.'"

"This tone seems too unlike the Avenar we know," I say.

"What do you mean?"

"Do not discount the possibility of force. Avenar could not have been alone when these words were written."

Her eyes widen and her voice deepens to ruby. "If what you say is true, dear Rehsotis, then it is even worse than I could imagine. Then Our Blessed Mother has been betrayed."

With that she goes into her chamber and does not emerge for days, and she sends no courier back with a letter of response.

When Avenar of Allepo rides a horse through the gateway of the convent, dark linen robes hang heavy across his broad shoulders. He dismounts and walks with deliberate steps into our midst. His dark eyes regard us with familiar intensity, but they do not sparkle. Abbess Carmelia greets him with open arms and takes him by the arm into the vineyard. Hours later they emerge, walking beside each other but not touching. As he hoists himself back up unto the back of his horse, he looks around at all of us.

"Sisters, I come to warn you. The bishop demands some allegiance to the efforts of the Church. He urges you to adhere to the tenants and orders of the Church as issued by the pope. Imprudence will not serve any of you well. I urge you to bear upon your abbess in these matters. And so you know. Those who wish to are welcome to journey to my sanctuary where your safety will be ensured."

He rides away through the gate. For a long time, Abbess Carmelia stares after him and the point at which he disappears into the forest. Without speaking I go to her and escort her into the Gathering Hall where she leads us through morning songs.

Our rhythm is regained in the moon tides that follow. We do not speak of Avenar of Allepo again. No one leaves to join him.

* * *

Their sails match the red sunset. When Abbess Carmelia and I see them approaching, she takes one look at me and I nod to affirm her worst fears: Boats filled with Smallheaded approach. Large crosses on the front sail in bold gold sharpened by wide black borders declare these Smallheaded's agency: They are the bishop's mercenaries.

Abbess Carmelia calls to the others to not ask questions, but to gather our belongings—all we could carry—and without hesitation go into hiding in the forest. It does not take us long. Our tidiness and sense of order makes it easy to put the dearest of our manuscripts onto carts, roll tapestries from the walls, hoist packs of food upon our backs, and help the infirm to walk between our strong shoulders. Before the sun is at its highpoint, we leave the convent and hurry through the poppy fields into the shelter of the woods.

They gain shore at night, during a birthing moon. They make their way from the beach, in a light too dim to cast distinct shadows. But they surprise no one. We all are gone by the time the marauders reach the convent.

For several nights we hide within the shadows and gullies of the woods. Into the high canopy of the dense oaks, we hoist tapestry hammocks where our most ill can rest silent and secure. Others hide within canopies constructed of collected fir limbs. We hear the cries and yells of the assailants as they pillage the convent. Flames from the burning buildings lick the night sky. When the wood frames burn, the limestone walls collapse into mounds like bones, ribs scattered, rings of spine strewn over an ash carpet. None of them venture into the forest searching for us. Their purpose is not murder, but intimidation.

The bishop wants Abbess Carmelia's fear and recalcitrance; but he ill understands her heart and mind, her passion. Even before the flames subside to amber, before the wailing and weeping of the sisters and pilgrims ease into the sobs of disbelief, he had lost her. She never belonged to him. I watch her face as we stand a safe distance from the convent walls. She holds her shoulders straight. Her eyes are clear. She takes the hands of those closest to her and leads us back to the ruined convent, the spent poppies yielding against our legs.

In the air all around the convent, gray curtains of ash glitter in suspension for several days; we uncover and gather all the salvageable and untouched portions of our lives. The marauders stripped only the visible treasures we had not carried away: the largest finished tapestries, the boxes of dyes and inks, thick leather-bound volumes filled with gold and blue illuminations, the decanted bottles of distilled night from the poppies—these they stole away. But they had not found and opened the cool recesses beneath the convent's floors, where we stored well-seasoned cheese coated in roasted herbs, amphorae of daily wine and oil, and baskets of roasted grain. We find several volumes unburned and whole on the floor of the scriptorium in the Hall of Learning. Some of the spoons and knives left in the Gathering Hall can still be used.

We clear space in the Common Hall and gather together, looking to Abbess Carmelia for word of what to do next. We share our meal, we wrap ourselves in comforting robes, and Abbess Carmelia reads to us from the codices she salvaged from her own shelves, her strong voice like a ship into which we climb amidst the moldering desecration.

We are glad the spring is early and warm, and we make a practical camp near the fallen convent walls. Many of the sisters do nothing but sleep for days. Among those of us who work to salvage and clear the convent's ruins, little is said—such unfamiliar silence among the sisters when working together. Many leave, in frustration and grief, to return to their villages and homes. By the next full moon, only a dozen of us carry on together.

We gather around the light of a fire around which all life circulates. I recall those seasons in the mere chamber with Yenheth and Grendel, my time with Yargis and the brothers. Onions and smoked rabbit roast in the hot fire. The swallows dip and pip above our heads, as if nothing has changed, as if nothing is about to happen.

"We cannot stay here. You cannot stay here." Abbess Carmelia sends discomforting ripples through the air with her words. Only a rising cloud of cricket trills mingles with the smoke of the fire and fragrance of cooking food.

"But shouldn't we rebuild, Abbess? We cannot, certainly, abandon our home. I hardly know another." The murmurs of the others supported Sister Agatha's suggestion. "The bishop cannot strike us down so easily."

"You are no longer safe." Abbess Carmelia measures her tone. "I will not hold any of you in a place where you could come again so close to harm. And harm will come again. For days I have meditated, wanting first to rebuild, as you urged. I too, at first, wanted us to rise up like another season here—in this place I know as home. As we all know as home. But you all must understand—I will not ask that of you. Most have already ventured back, hoping and praying Our

Blessed Mother will bring them to a safe place. You must all consider that, pray about it, take it into your hearts."

"But I have no place I would rather be." Sister Agatha persists.

"If we rebuild," interrupts Abbess Carmelia, "the bishop will believe it an insult, a mockery, a challenge. He will not allow us to continue in endeavors inharmonious with his intentions."

"With his ambitions, you mean." Sister Agatha's voice shakes. "So let us challenge him. He does not follow the way. You know he does not let the Spirit of the Creator guide his actions. He mocks Our Blessed Mother. Wants to put a male god at the center."

"And do I presume to claim a deeper truth? How do you know he is not equally driven by a profound conviction as strong as mine? I know the Christ in one way. He knows the Creator in his. He believes in his way with as much devotion and certainty as we believe in ours."

"Yes, but he has the power of the pope at his back. And we now see what he is able to do with that advocacy." Sister Agatha turns to look at those who remain at the convent.

"Know this," Abbess Carmelia raises an open hand to silence other objections, "I will not engage in a conflict fueled by the bishop's hubris. I do not need to stake a claim, Sister. I want only to hear the voice of my creator and Our Blessed Mother. Her voice, here and now, is silent to me. I cannot find her. She has departed and I will follow. If the bishop is so desperate to stop me, he will not desist until he has succeeded. You are right—he is backed by enforcements from secular powers I do not have. And if I try to tap the support of those who love us, who believe in us and in our ties to all good and true things, we will put them also at risk.

"The bishop believes he not only does the Creator's will, but the will of the pope. And it brings him gifts and power of his own, and now he craves more of the same. It is a new structure of governance, but it is strong. It promises a way without thought. You and I and all the dear ones gathered here believe the Christ did not want us to stop with our questions. But the bishop wants us to do only his bidding.

He is imposing his will, not the will of God and Our Blessed Mother. If we do not do his will... this is what happens." Abbess Carmelia stops, her face gleaming with her tears.

"But Abbess..." Sister Agatha takes hold of Abbess Carmelia's arms.

"Dear, dear Sister. All of you. I will not stay. You may choose to do as you wish. Make your heart's choice. But I will not force any course of action upon you. I am decided."

"I shall go with you." I hardly recognize my voice.

"Dear Sister Rehsotis, are you certain?"

"Even before you began to speak."

"Then let us make ready. We will leave as soon as a suitable craft can be built."

* * *

Conversations such as these fill every evening. They are debates at first, then gentle discussions where Sister Carmelia urges the sisters to remain strong in their decisions and not let their hearts fail them. They decide to stay with Sister Agatha.

We build our raft with the help of the sisters who choose to remain, a craft large enough for the two of us to be comfortable—not as simple as a raft, and not as elegant as a barge. The rectangular frame is fashioned from four straight and strong felled oak saplings from the woodland. We weave lengths of hickory and leather upon the frame, and over this platform we secure a hut of jute and tapestry. A small sail is set and rigged. Several paddles and poles are trimmed and planed from light and strong ironwood.

The boat is finished upon a full moon. The sea is gentle and inviting. We pack satchels of supplies to carry from the convent into the next part of our lives. At morning, Sister Agatha and her small company wish us farewell at the shore, and we push off, heavy with provisions and longing—Abbess Carmelia and me.

* * *

We drift toward the Island of the Brothers. It is not fate, so much as the strength of the currents and the press of the wind. I recognize the high rock skellig as we pull the boat to the calm northwest harbor where, ages ago, I rolled into the arms of the brothers. Remembered voices overcome my spirit as we land and make our way up the steps to the island's crest. Abbess Carmelia walks beside me, leaning upon my arm. We gain the top and find only silence: hollow mounds, hollow huts, all abandoned. I feel a shattering within me.

When our gazes meet, tears fill our eyes. I sense her thoughts brimming with questions. The cross still occupies its crowning location in the settlement. We climb to it and stand there for a long time. I resist an impulse to kneel, although Abbess Carmelia eases herself down to her knees, presses her head against the center of the cross, and murmurs a low and sonorous string of prayers. When she at last falls silent, I tremble.

"Here is where I will stay."

"No. There is too much pain lingering here."

Abbess Carmelia bows her head as if to ask for blessing and forgiveness. I do not have either to offer.

"You are ill. Sick with grief and fever. You nursed me to health. Let me do the same for you here, and then we will make our way back to the mainland. Let me take you to Avenar of Aleppo's sanctuary."

"I will hear none of that." She grasps the edge of the cross to brace herself up.

"But part of what makes you ill is your heart sickness. When you go to him, with you near, he will be able to see the truth behind the bishop's lies. There are no other sisters depending upon you now. See this as your Blessed Mother permitting you to do what your heart burns to do."

"I will not. You may call it pride. And so be it. But I shall not capitulate in any way."

"But he will not see it as that, certainly. He could not know how far the bishop has gone until you tell him what was brought down upon us."

I know I speak the truth, but she will not believe me.

"I am at journey's end. But you have far to go. Leave me alone with my Creator and Our Blessed Mother, Sister Rehsotis. You are done here. Let me find my way to my beloved without the limits of this flesh."

"That is the fever speaking."

"No. It is what I choose to do, and from you I have learned it is possible. Go. Now. I have provisions. The seas are still calm. You do not need to stay. I do not want you to stay. Go and find him. This Yargis for whom you called out during your own fever."

I make my way back down those hundreds of steps, stumbling through my tears, and launch the small craft into the sea. As the prevailing winds bring me around to the north of the skellig, I see her standing at its rocky cross-marked crest. We watch each other until there is nothing of us to be seen, and then for hours beyond, my eyes focus on the spot where I know she probably still remains, resting against the stone cross, her face turned east, toward Avenar, toward the rising sun.

PART FOUR

VILLAGE

There are voices at sea.

As I drift, my mind fills with the images and words of all I knew before. But there are other entities clamoring to be recognized. I awaken during the early weeks of this solitary passage, usually at night, moon full, phosphorescent life teeming all around me, as if a glowing and ecstatic dream carries my boat to my destination. I dip my hands into the pulsing waves, rich in creatures briny to the taste. After eating my fill from the boat's store of food, I lap fresh water from the hollows and crannies of the craft and wash my cheeks and lips clean. Then I turn and fold into myself again; I return to the other self of hibernation, each time falling deeper and longer into timelessness.

* * *

Hibernation suspends more than the functions of the body. Long I drift suspended in a place without context. The sun and moon draw the only line through those years, and this is a relief. I listen to my breath as if it were the breeze, the waves, another rhythm residing both within and outside of my body. I do not own it. It possesses me. My breath presses me against a canvas of darkness. No light, yet there are distinct shadows. Darkness is gradated and toned with blue-black and

141

green-black. And in this state, sound and color add tactile awareness of what is now cool, now warm. I inhabit a muffled world, float above it, then below it, sometimes wrapping around it. I am being carried in the womb of my mother: an awareness of all that touches and moves her. For me the sea becomes the Mother—and She infuses my world. Sometimes Her thoughts stumble, for She knows something shifts, but nothing makes Her certain of me. She carries me—a long gestation during which I knock about in Her salty currents. Countless seasons. Innumerable moons.

* * *

The currents around me shift and change their rhythm. Their moon dance alters my course several times. I arrive upon the shore, awake fully, and push myself yet again into the grounded world. I wander far inland and find a freshwater spring from which I drink, as if tasting a secret. Not far from it, I find a steaming pool pulsing from a hidden underground source; I ease into the warm waters and bathe softness back into my limbs, face, and hair. The verdant layered lace of quillwort and cress grow within reach. Their tender moss flavors settle my empty stomach. I wash my linen cloaks and dry them in the sun. Warmed and fed, I dress, satchel my belongings, and make my way into the landscape that seems familiar yet vague as a recurring dream.

I walk for several days, stopping only to eat. I come upon a village during dawn, and the scent of baking bread and a melody from a high, tremulous voice draws me closer to a circle of earth and stone huts. The song includes words I recognize from my mother Anathian tongue. My heart races at the possibility of finding a gathering of Anathians, even though nothing of our scent or thoughts opens to me. Hope rests like a lozenge upon my tongue as I stumble and run toward the wood fire scent, the music of familiar language.

The woman bending at the fire turns to me as I come into the center of the quiet village. She is not Anathian, but there is a kindred spark in her wideset amber eyes. She stands as tall as I, and she blinks in amazement when she sees me.

"Keeper? Are you returned to us?"

"I am not Keeper. My name is Rehsotis."

She studies my face for a long time and nods. "I am Lunak. You are not Keeper, but you are of his kind." She speaks my language, although it is obscured by an unfamiliar accent.

"What do you mean? Why do you say I am of his kind?"

"You speak with old and some familiar tones, Dear One. How far have you journeyed to find us here?" Her voice is a shimmering pool filled with sleekly silver fish.

I crumble. Wrenching and unexpected sobs shake my body and drop me to my knees. Without another word, Lunak holds me and rocks me with comforting murmurs. She helps me gain my feet, leads me closer to the village's common fire, where she eases me down upon a thick cushion. As others gather around, murmuring soft questions and comments, she brings me a gourd of a pleasantly bitter syrup and a small crusty loaf of barley bread.

I learn about these Akkara, who like my own Anathian, moved often to avoid conflict and war with the Smallheaded. We have in common ancient ancestors. Although many of her words and the words of her fellows are uttered in a different cadence and tone, we find our tongues rooted in similar words and meanings.

I try to listen more than speak, but I ache to learn more about the one like me they call Keeper. That evening, after being coddled and fed by the Akkara, I turn to Lunak. "Please, tell me about Keeper."

She takes my hand and leads me to a small hut. Our shoulders are level and her grasp is strong.

"We will share this space until you decide what you mean to do." She offers a seat on a long thick cushion along the side wall and sets a lantern next to me. "Wait here."

When she returns, she holds a thick scroll of vellum. "Here. I think you will be able to make this out well enough to understand.

It is part of the story of our tribe, the part most recent, about when Keeper came to us."

I unroll the sheets as if they are made of petals and find that I indeed can decipher the words I find inscribed in violet ink. Small sketches and drawings illustrate the story. An acrid, smoky fragrance wafts from the pages, enhancing the near trance I fall into as I read the words. Line by line I realize Keeper is Yargis, healer and teller of tales. He made his way here after the Island of the Brothers. This place of the Akkara, not so far from my own long-ago home, is only several moons of travel north of where Grendel and my mother Yenheth died. When I turn to the last page, across the top is a tenderly wrought drawing of my beloved. And below it are inscribed the words:

> Keeper, who calls himself Yargis. Much loved by those of our village of the Akkara. Came to us weak and ill. Grew strong and lived with us for many years. His heart remained sad and never healed. He was waiting and what he waited for never arrived. After hundreds of seasons, Keeper died with caring healers attending. His last word: *Raysotiss*.

* * *

The night sky above the village is domed by sheets of flowing amethyst and topaz light. The colors breathe, animated by their own power of green, red, violet, and blue, and, most often, a dazzling white, all humming against the pitch of darkness. In this village of the Akkara, I find welcome as if I were a long-awaited friend.

The Akkara are as proud as the Anathians. Their rich land yields abundance and plenty, and they devote time in peaceful attendance to their ancestors, the examination of their souls, and the application of their dreams. They raise their children. Thrive. In the forested hills surrounding their village, they gather edible and medicinal herbs and roots. From these they distill purple dyes for the soft leather they tan from the hides of deer and bear. From strong hemp and reeds they fashion rope and paper. They fish the streams and lakes. Their herd of goats produces rich milk. And within an octagon-walled hut, contented doves lay eggs and sometimes are culled for meat. Their ancient, accomplished magic includes dream-gliding and even transformation.

The largest structure in the village is called The Holding. Baskets hang from the walls and lean along the edge of the spacious hall; scrolls cram these baskets and upon them are written their history, rituals, designs, songs, and fancies. This library is organized and watched over by Tambor, the tribal leader and story keeper.

Lunak explains how Tambor's spirit passes from one generation to the next; when one body dies, Tambor's soul passes into the next-born child. Although most of the Akkara's stories and knowledge are written down, the living Tambor holds it all within the mind and heart. Tambor is not considered either male or female, but neutral; and all in the tribe are its mates and companions.

As we talk into the night, I learn of how the first Tambor was born during a flood. "One spring, the rains began and did not stop for several moons," Lunak says, lighting an evening pipe of sweet-scented herbs. "The Akkara were desperate and frightened. Our huts were washed away. We were forced to climb into the high reaches of giant chestnut trees, the waters chasing us ever higher. A woman named Kuhn was great with child and even as the rising river lapped at the soles of her feet, labor gripped her and her own waters burst to mingle with the dark, rising water. Her lover wrapped himself around her, holding her safe in the tree like a human sling. 'Do not be afraid,' he called to her, above the roar of the rushing flood. Again and again, he called to her to not be afraid, and she listened and grew to love him even more. At last, the child slipped from Kuhn's womb and into the waiting nest of the father's belly. And when the babe gasped and cried out, the rain stopped. It ceased at the very moment of the child's first breath. The sky cleared and a banner of colors stretched above their heads. And as the infant wailed, full of life and vigor, the waters receded. The Akkara knew this child and its spirit were of the river. Its spirit eternal, always changing, but ever present and ready to rise again."

* * *

With the Akkara, I spend much of my time in The Holding and read again and again their transcribed history, especially of the time they shared with Yargis. From it I draw comfort. Here I learn his remains were disposed of in the Akkara fashion, so similar to the Anathian way. Only instead of releasing the body into the sea on the funeral pyre, the Akkara reduce their dead to ash on a common spot, the pyre rebuilt for each use, with the ashes of one commingling with the remains of those who preceded them.

I ask Lunak to take me to the common pyre. She leads me along a path through a dense grove of burr oak. The sound of rushing water grows louder as I follow her, and we come upon a small glade at the side of a thin waterfall streaming over the surface of red stone. In the center of the circular glade rises charred rocks the size of large baskets encircling the time-compressed ash of the dead Akkara.

"We brought him here." Her words sound as if they are played upon a lyre. "His remains were added to the generations of Akarra who died before." She leaves me alone in the glade and walks back to the village.

With each step a prayer, I enter the funeral pit and stretch out upon the ash bed. Above me clouds tussle with the breeze against the cobalt sky. Images of Yargis' last days wash over me. I see his body prepared for the funeral pyre. I stand with the Akarra who loved him. I add my song of mourning to theirs.

At last I know.

I have found him. I do not know why he left me, but I know he was waiting for me.

* * *

Decades of mourning follow. Lunak dies. I watch her children grow to nurture children of their own, and then their children and theirs, generations nested like shells into the next generation.

And always Tambor. For hundreds of years, the village's current Tambor and I are there, to recall and foretell.

Each night Tambor and I tell stories of our pasts and address each other with a question, sometimes one of nonsense, sometimes of poetry. What is the color of the wind? What do fish dream? How many languages do trees speak? How often does the river exhale? How many facets of color are in the eyes of God?

* * *

In the spring-fed lake near the Akkara village, I dive several lengths of my body deep and do not touch the bottom. Thoughts of the sea pound into my temples and fill my heart. When I emerge, Tambor sits at the shore. I bend to gather my robes and cover my nakedness.

"Do not be ashamed."

"I am not ashamed. I am only surprised."

"It is pleasing to watch you swim. It is pleasing to look at you." With that, Tambor rises and leaves. I stand, rooted at the shore, and watch the slow departure and try to grasp some trailing thread of thought. But Tambor's mind is closed to me.

I join Tambor and a few others around the fire that evening, as is custom. With clarity and keen recall of lifetime upon lifetime, Tambor shares long stories of their tribe, of battles fought and never lost, of their ultimate battle, which ended all conflict for ages.

"How do you know it was the last conflict?" This is not one of our questions for simple amusement. I want to crack open the pod of his confidence.

Tambor sits back on his cushion. "This time in peace has been long. There is room for even more. As long as our numbers are constant, and the boundaries of our lives and the rest of the creation maintain a harmony, we shall live in comfort."

"I want to believe you. But my own heritage, and my history with the myths, dreams, and truths of so many tribes, lead me to caution you. This could be another fragile illusion."

147

On this night, Tambor, having drunk more than a little of the first wine, pulls me away from the others. "I know why you are so sad. You retell all stories of your life, your kind, but you have not told the story of Keeper since you first arrived. Indeed, only the ancient grandmother Lunak knew of your connection to him. He is why you are so sad.

"I have never told you this," Tambor's breath is mellow with wine, "but I can be him—for you."

"What do you mean? Pretend to 'be him?' Because you know so much about him, do you think you can reenact his gestures, recreate his touch?"

For so long I have managed to dance away from the images and recollections of Yargis, and now they are called forth, pushing through the fabric of memory like sharp blades.

"When I saw you at the lake today, I knew. You have hidden too well. You found him here—but you did not say farewell. I would not be pretending. I can become him for you. Only once. I can perform it only once in any of my body's lifetime, and it does not last long. The magic is that powerful. I offer this to you. All you need to do is ask and it shall be done."

"How long does such magic last?" I take a step back from the charged air surrounding Tambor.

"A short while. Perhaps nearly a day. It will depend upon my strength, the force of your encounter. That is part of the risk. You may ache more in yearning after than you do now."

For days, I ponder the gift. I take what Tambor said, and hold it like Yargis' burning glass up to the light. In the centuries since I last knew Yargis in the flesh, I have known much warmth. The comforts of love from our daughter Illisante, the friendship of the brothers, the affection of the children at the convent, the companionship of the sisters and Abbess Carmelia, and the respect and esteem of the Akkara. But I have not been touched, held, or caressed as a woman in all that time. I try to imagine the sensation of his arms around me, but cannot. I want to hear the sound, even a whisper, of his voice. My heart becomes entangled in the possibility of once again inhaling his spicy skin. The prospect of being with my beloved again is potent.

I grow silent around the common fire for many nights. Tambor continues to tell grand stories of the Akkara's past, but I do not contribute my own tales. I do not answer or ask our regular, nocturnal questions; they now seem nonsensical, superfluous, and intolerable. I am not interested in debating how long it took a mountain to grow, when a child begins to forget her birth journey, or why we are compelled to create things of beauty only to later destroy them. All I think about is the possibility to be with Yargis again.

Upon finishing the story, Tambor waits until the others leave the fire, turns to me and bows, a reminder that the invitation holds. After each incitement, I turn and walk away. The question I hold unresolved in my heart: "Would the pain upon parting again be more painful than the first?'

The loneliness is so intense I can taste it—vinegar and salt. My tears. I have not wept for years, and now the tears come uninvited and unremitting. I sit far from Tambor; my sobs are silent and more wrenching because of that.

When the others turn to their huts and their own dreams, I go to Tambor. We bow to each other in turn.

"Wait for me then, in your hut. I shall be there presently."

I prepare for the unknown. I comb my hair as if it were a song. I massage oil infused with cardamom, lavender, and fennel into my arms and legs, and around my hips and across my shoulders I drape a silk mantle dyed rich in tones of cinnabar and azure. Over my sleeping pallet I spread a soft tapestry created with the sisters; it is covered with a meandering pattern of life woven with threads colored by dyes made from moss, bark, and blood; it evokes the summer fields around the convent. I light a lamp filled with olive oil. I chew a root of licorice. Then I stand in the middle of my hut and wait.

At last, Tambor raps at my door. I open it.

"Follow me." Tambor carries a small bowl in his right hand, the moon's reflection caught in its liquid contents. My own right hand fits into Tambor's left, and together we walk to the communal funeral pyre. Tambor and I stop at the foot of the pyre's blackened remains.

"Hold out your arms, with your hands cupping up, against each other."

I do so.

Tambor closes his eyes and his voice thrums. "Mijn geliefd. Ik roep aan u. Aangezien u van me in het leven hield zla k me nu herinneren. Laat onze harten worden verfreist."

The pile of ash shifts as if someone blows upon it and crisscrossing lines appear over its the surface.

"This time say it with me."

Together we repeat, "My beloved, I call to you. As you loved me in life, shall I now remember. Let our hearts be refreshed."

The ashes shift again, then swirl and reach like a willow tree into the moonstruck night. We repeat the phrases again, until one glittering strand of ashes separates from the rest, turns purple, and spirals toward me. As a snake of amethyst crystals, it twines around my arms, up around my neck, down my torso and legs, around my ankles, back up my body, and across my shoulders. It flows into my cupped hands, where it coils and contracts into a tight ball. The color dims until I hold only ashes, which I sift like valuable coins through my fingers into the bowl Tambor holds out to me.

Stirring the ashes into the contents of the bowl, Tambor calls, "*Deze as wordt me. Ik word deze as.*" This ash becomes me. I become this ash.

After drinking from the bowl, Tambor passes it to me. "Here. Drink all that you can until you need to take a breath. And then drink some more."

I gasp and swallow, and we pass the bowl between us until its contents are gone. Tambor strokes the lingering ash from the bottom of the bowl and wipes it over my eyelids, down my nose, across my lips and against my ears. I do the same in return. Tambor leads me away from the fire back to my hut. When we are inside, the ash mixture on my skin begins to burn, and I reach up to wipe it from my face.

"You must not. The sensations will pass, you must not. Here, hold my hands."

My stomach spasms and wrenches, and I am overcome with the unfamiliar sensation of nausea.

"Tambor, I feel ill, very ill. Perhaps this is not the same for my kind. Perhaps I am not able to tolerate this." I whimper with the next swell of discomfort.

"All is happening as it should. All is as expected."

Tambor's own face contorts and twists in agony. Grasping each other's hands, we bend over and struggle to ride through the sensation of hot pitch rising along our spines. We break free from each other and fall to the floor, bodies rippling with convulsions. I reach for Tambor and find no mooring body.

"Close your eyes. Do not open them until all is quiet. Not until then." The words are knobbed like cedar roots thrusting from the earth.

I shut my eyes, fall to my knees, and roll into a wash of fire and darkness. I hear Tambor's cries of anguish, but it is as if a waterfall rushes between us.

Like a door, the curtain of transformation swings open. I am tossed down upon the ground, the pain falling off me like a shell. Again, I hear the cicada staccato the night and the soft drift of the breeze dallies.

Next to me, the deep breathing of my companion.

I open my eyes, and Yargis stretches alongside me. He rolls over and gazes at me, and I fall into the warmth of his golden eyes.

"Is it you? Truly, really you?"

Without a word, Yargis pulls me to him, and I taste the smoky salt of his mouth.

"I am here." He stands and lifts me to my feet.

"Shall we go to the lake? The sea is too far from here."

He laughs a low, chesty rumble of pleasure, a sound so treasured. "My dear Rehsotis. We do not need the sea." He leads me over to the tapestry-covered pallet where I unlace his cloak from his shoulders and pull open his robe while he unwraps the silk mantle from my arms and waist. He folds me into his arms, and I wrap mine around him, and the terrible sense of longing breaks open and falls away.

With lips and fingertips, we revisit the landscapes of each other's bodies. Certainly mine is changed, but his is just as I remember it. With my tongue, I trace the length of his jaw, the sweep of his neck. His tongue tracks the line of my teeth, the base of my throat. My nose dances against the flex of his thighs, around the shaft of his cock. His lips travel across my abdomen, count each rib, and linger long at my breasts. My tongue savors the slope of his spine, and his circles my knees, and with a breath, he parts my legs. I suck each of his fingers and find them tender-jointed. He caresses the small of my back, the arches of my feet. I trace the fine map of veins along his forearms and tangle my fingers in his silken hair. I inhale his scent of sage and clove. He breathes me in, and I do not disappear.

This is Yargis—his face, mouth, jaw, neck, thighs, groin, spine, fingers, arms, hair. His scent. His voice. His flavor. Alive.

We roll over and around each other as if we were together again in the sea. Our skin glistens with sweat. Our eyes gleam bright. I laugh when, at last, I press him back against the pallet and ease myself down upon his hips, not wanting to rush toward that first climax, but unable to wait any longer. We greedily feed each other's hunger, while gentling each other's yearning.

For the first time in centuries, I am warm to my marrow.

When we grow hungry, we share a common cup of wine, tear open a pomegranate, and feed each other its bittersweet seeds. We roast figs and apricots on sticks above the fire, let them cool, spread them open, and smooth their yielding hearts over each other's shoulders, breasts and hips, and then savor each other clean of the fruit's rich flesh. We hold each other when we rest amidst our lovemaking, and while still within each other's arms, we talk about all that has happened.

"When you found me, I thought my death was imminent. And then, you returned me to life. Such transformation." He presses his forehead against mine. "When you went to tell the brothers we were leaving, I thought it would be best for me to go ahead and find a safe place. I did not want us to wander. Especially with you carrying our child."

"You knew?" I hold him more tightly. "Of course you knew. How could you not know? But why didn't you tell me?"

He leans back to look at me fully. "Not tell you? What do you mean? I left a letter. Upon the table under the goblets."

"I found no letter. There was nothing. Nothing but your absence. And months of trying to find you in my dreams. All empty. All vacant." I trace that time in my mind, try to see the table, to wonder how I would have missed his message. "Could Brother Angus have found the letter? He did not want us united. He certainly did not want anything that would have resulted from our coupling."

The weight of speculation bears down upon us. And with it comes the clarity of right instinct.

"I gave up too soon."

"No, no. My dearest. We kept searching. Too often the way toward that which we most long for is obscured by the depth of our desire. And I did sense you searching. I knew you were trying to make your way to me. The failure is as much mine, not holding on a while longer. Long enough, at least, for you to reach me.

"But you have found me," he whispers his wonderment. "And in all this time, you are the one about whom I thought. The one for whom I yearned."

We weave tight around each other—our flesh, our dreams, our breath, our laughter. As the moon rises in the next night, I sense that the visitation is ending. As I kiss him, yet again, I taste a little less salt. His lips slowly cooled. We regard each other, and I fight away tears.

We hold each other and my heart pounds against the drum of his chest "You must close your eyes." His words are distilled wishes. "Rest here with me, close your eyes, and do not open them until you hear the nightingale. I am leaving you, and in the morning, my host Tambor will remember none of this time together."

I cling to him until he pulls away gentle as moss, kisses my eyelids and my lips one last time. The door of my hut rattles open and latches shut. Then silence. So much silence. Even when the long-fluted notes of the nightingale's song reach me, I do not open my eyes.

That evening, I search Tambor's face for some sort of sign. He recognizes me as Rehsotis, but not as the lover of Yargis. As Yargis told me, this is Tambor, and only Tambor.

"You are not sad?"

"It was a blessing to be with him."

"No regrets?"

I stop and roll the question around in my mind like a smooth stone. I wait for a pang of sorrow, but none comes. "I expect it will renew my grief, but it will not wrench and tear me apart as much as the first time. This time, I know we did not abandon each other. This time will be different."

"As I expect it will be for you, dear friend."

* * *

Tonight the moon is full. I study its face as if it were an epistle filled with longed-for answers. It offers a bas-relief of a woman's face. She is there, looking down at me, her face calm and ready with untold stories. Around her neck hangs an ink-stone talisman. The Akkara and I gather around the evening fire and the moon trembles and fragments of its surface seem to fall away and crumble. Our stories and songs hang in the air unfinished, and the wolves in the distance bay and wail as never before. Even the doves awaken and flush out of their dovecote.

Tambor raises his staff. "Something is altered. Take shelter. In the morning, all will be clearer."

154

But the morning sun is dim and crosses a sky of perpetual gray. And so it is for many days. At the midst of the growing season, the bean pods do not swell and the plum blossoms fall from their fruity promise. The Akkara must tap their reserves. New rituals are created and offered, but their magic is not strong enough and the sky does not clear. We live for several seasons in perpetual fog as our stores are depleted. Tambor spends nights sleepless, confused and uncertain.

* * *

The air is laden with the scent of fire steel striking against stone. Just as I begin to believe we are more similar than different, a warrior band of Smallheaded is upon us. Again they bring illness and destruction, their malevolence and greed palpable. I did not notice the omens. Long years of deep friendship with the Akkara made me oblivious to the coming evil signified in the change of air, my dreams increasingly thick and heavy with the gray clouds of their approach, the wrenching sobs that would overtake me without warning or reason—all of these should have spoken to me of their arrival. I could have warned them. I could have kept us all safe a little while longer.

So when I see the Smallheaded's pinched faces, their teeth dark, their breath dank, a wave of death washes upon me. We are defenseless.

* * *

A solitary mourning dove calls to the golden evening. There is no reply. Her lonely fluted notes echo again and again against the thickening night. There is a hive of many years in the low hollow of a long-dying beech tree. The honey is cold and dark amber; its chambers crumble in my mouth—waxen remnants of summer in the midst of this late winter forest. How Tambor will savor the taste. I fill a small basket with several dripping sections of the comb, and we will pass it around the story ring, each of the Akkara taking a portion, leaving enough for the spirits. And that portion will be tossed into the fire—a flaring, waxy offering to the star-netted night. We will be ready for the Smallheaded.

* * *

The seasons that follow are too familiar to me. The Smallheaded settle not far from the village. The Akkara keep peace for a short time. The invading Smallheaded do not conserve their supplies or know how to replenish them. After just one season of drought—one of many to come for which the Akkara predicted and prepared—the Smallheaded suffer and they plunder our storehouses. Then they return, demanding more and accusing us that we are hiding stores of food.

Tambor tells them we all are gripped in the same state of loss, but they believe we have unopened hoards of goods. They do not believe Tambor's stories of our many failed crops. They do not believe the entire passage of seasons is changing. Nothing will grow as it has in the past, and the once healthy sleek deer and spiny spiked boar we hunt will continue to grow more thin and forlorn.

Tambor urges peaceful cooperation. But I know such breath is wasted.

* * *

After Tambor meets again with the leaders of the band of Smallheaded, I am startled from my sleep by the image of Tambor's grimacing face. I arise and race to the dwelling hut, but I am too late. Three Smallheaded push past me as they flee into the night. They have cut Tambor's throat clean and deep. My friend lies dead in a pool of crimson blood. Grief tears at us.

Tambor arrives in my dreamscape three nights after the murder, with a face still covered in blood, eyes blinded by the blows suffered at the hands of the Smallheaded.

In my dream, Tambor's words are clear: "Destroy The Holding and its contents. Do not allow our collected wisdom to fall into misguided and ill hands. Now. Rehsotis. Awaken now, set everyone running safe into the woods, and then burn it all to the ground. Take the ash and work it into our beloved soil until there is not a trace of it. Let only the land remember."

"You are wrong. If we do, there will not be a testimony of your having been here. You and the Akkara will be forgotten, utterly forgotten. Do not let these invaders reduce your story to a few shards. That would be the greatest of sorrows. I know of what I speak. All evidence of my own tribe has been lost. All that I have of what was once a grand Labyrinth is a small piece of stone not much larger than a seed. And here you call for me to remove all evidence of your finest accomplishments. Consider what you are asking."

The spirit image grows larger before answering my plea. "I would rather have our history lost than allow it to be turned into a curiosity, a myth about which others will speculate, an intellectual amusement. Please do as I ask of you."

I cannot refuse my friend this request. In the middle of the night, I wake my companions and tell them to leave in silence. When I tell them about the Tambor's visit, they do not protest. I make my way to The Holding, and with wailing and tears, set it to blaze. At first, even the fire resists its nature, as if horrified by what it is expected to commit in the name of something akin to honor. But the fire cannot resist its true nature, and its blue-edged red tongue laps at the baskets and the scrolls. The diaries and journals of the teachers, the priests, the seers—I pull them from baskets and off shelves and feed them to the fire. The long rolls of ancient tales and name-tracing histories gleam red around the edges, curl like a broken-necked bird, and lift wings of grief into the night. And smoldering beneath them, the thick table-sized volumes, bound by glistening, gossamer threads, containing the charms, incantations, and recipes proven and tested by centuries of use. The small testaments and dream books—all burn and fly into the wind like many-winged moths. Soon all that offered witness to the Akkara is gone.

The fire spreads from The Holding to the other common houses and the dwelling huts. But before all crumbles, I commit one act in defiance of Tambor's final wishes. Just as the flames are about to catch hold and fast, I grasp the scroll of the Akkara's history containing the story of Yargis. In the woods where the Akkara have fled, I seek out a long-descended daughter of Lunak, press the scroll into her arms, and tell her to keep it with her, no matter what happens. I tell her that when she comes near the end of her life, she must pass the scroll on to her daughter, or any other nearest of her kin, sharing the promise to keep the scroll safe—one solitary, extant manuscript for the next generation of Akkara. And one small way to keep the name Yargis in the world.

The band of Akkara heads north.

I turn south.

In dreams that follow, I watch as the few remaining Akkara drift away on rafts of ice, their tall silhouettes clear against the night sky of dancing lights of chattering blue and undulating wine-warm red.

* * *

In self-imposed exile from any resembling the Smallheaded, I survive. Subsist. Sometimes I come upon a small village of others like the Akkara; I hide from them. Time spreads like a web of dark shadow, where elements of self—breath, sleep, taste—catch like errant moths. Then one morning, numb with lack of intent or purpose, I stumble upon the edge of a large settlement of Smallheaded, the largest I have encountered. There are several rows of buildings built of stone and timber. Horses pull burdened carts and wagons over soil-packed roads. A wide river borders the western edge of the settlement, and along the eastern perimeter, silhouetted against the increasing light of morning, the tall masts of several sailing craft. I do not have the strength to run, and given the rising activity of the Smallheaded with the warming of the day, I crouch low and out of sight beneath the brush of the riverbank and watch and listen to the insect activity of the residents.

With evening I drift into a troubled, superficial sleep and stumble upon the dream of a Smallheaded sleeping not far from me. Her dream vibrates to my bones, and it pulls me to where she lives—a large, cast-off rate far at the back of one of the storehouses near the harbor, where she sells stolen creature-comforts: chocolate, coffee, thread, shoes, cooking oil, and small balls of opium. In her dream, another figure lurks. It is different from other dream presences—made more of shadow and memory and not immediate and current. It terrorizes her, and brings me fully awake. It is Anathian—after all these years, the remnant image of another like me.

I have to find this Smallheaded. Protected by the tall buildings' dark shadows, I make my way to her, covering my face with the deep hood of my dusty cloak.

In a leaning shack near the water's edge, I find her sleeping beneath several blankets. When I touch her shoulder, she jerks awake and in her eyes I find recognition.

"I am not the one you dream about." My voice is soft as the dark around us. "But I must know where the other is. Can you tell me?"

The whites of her eyes are thick with yellow mucus and her breath reeks from her rotting viscera. The scent of imminent death rises thick from her skin; she cries and whimpers and I cannot decipher her words, but they ring and twist the air with weariness and desperation. My own is overwhelming, and the sight of her fills me with a sour mixture of anger and sorrow. I see how both of us are pitiful creatures. She wails and curls at my feet, babbling about her own lost hopes and dreams. I gather her into my arms and rock her. Her sobs begin to quiet and then cease altogether. She does not struggle. I do not realize how tightly I hold her or when she stops breathing. Her face softens and resembles what she may have looked like as a young woman. Even a red and deep scar across her forehead becomes translucent. I have never found most Smallheaded beautiful, but in death this woman acquires a youthful comeliness. Gently I lay her down upon the many blankets in her hovel and leave her in peace.

For months after the encounter, I delve into deep sleep and glide from one dreaming soul to another, searching for some other fragment memory or encounter with others from my tribe. I long believe only distance or time keeps me from contact with others Anathian, and night after night, I search for some sign that I am not the last. But I do not find another Anathian refrain drifting in the dark—not even an echo.

PART FIVE

DEN

I sleep through most of the days. I would rather not, for my dreams become darker. More and more often I find myself back in the depths of the cave, bombarded by images of Grendel's bloodied victims, my mother Yenheth's arms reaching up in anger and sorrow. From those dreams I awake uneasy, look about my day's hiding place as if I expect either of them to step from my dream and into my world. I lie there, listening to my heart beating, and turn my thoughts to kinder ones, such as the lake's waves against the red rocks, the comfort of the soft forest floor, the scent of the warm earth.

I carry few possessions: Yargis's burning glass on its leather cord around my neck, my mother Yenheth's string of amber beads, linen cloaks and shifts, a knife and silver cup, and the handle of Beowulf's sword. It is rough with angry and uneven edges like a poorly healed wound. Yenheth's sword was more beautiful, its handle inscribed with runes detailing our first conflict with the Smallheaded and renderings of the creatures left behind by the Great Deluge. Upon one side of the handle was a minute and exquisite engraving of a band of Anathian dancing around the sun, the waters having receded, and the other creatures who survived the flood dancing with us. It was a time, according to our stories, when we believed we had survived, while the Smallheaded had not.

The river leads me north, deep into the land of years spent in peace with the Akkara; memories of their voices and songs fill the air around me. Having walked for weeks without stopping, I hunger for rest, a place to pause, and at last come upon this place, where I find a delicious quiet, touched at times with salt from the sea beyond the low ridge of mountains just to the east.

Dark-bellied clouds fill the sky. The forest is silent as every creature searches for warm cover before the storm. More snow. It smells like the sort with ice at its core. Small pellets that bite the skin and force you to keep eyes shut against the sting. If I were stronger, I would certainly journey to a place of continual warmth. I lived in such a place so briefly. A fragment of my time. If I conjure that memory now, and sleep, perhaps I can rest there, warm for at least a little while.

Here I did not see or sense any Smallheaded. Here the lake teams with fish so indolent, it is easy to catch them. I wash my garments in the stream and spread them over rocks to dry in the sun. Within the protection of a cluster of fir trees, I sleep. For the first time in months I am not awakened by nightmares.

When I arise I find my den, a snug but sufficient cave tucked at the foot of the hillside. I spend the shortening days turning it into a comfortable place, very like the sea chamber I shared with Yargis. Wild boar and deer provide bone, meat, and hides. From reeds and soft saplings, I weave seats and a sleeping pallet. The small goats of this land are a favorite of mine; they let me comb soft fur from their underbellies from which I twist soft cord to weave and knit. In a seasonal rhythm, I survive. The years pass.

* * *

One day a Smallheaded comes riding into my world. When I first see him, my impulse is to again gather my possessions and move. But he is quiet. Nearly transparent. He does little exploring but is, from what I observe, content with the fish he traps from the stream and the rations he brings with him for the summer season. He spends his waking hours devoted to constructing a small dwelling of logs. He finishes it just before the first frost, shutters the glass of the small windows, and rides away.

The next summer, and for many summers after it, he returns to live in his house, alone. He adds rooms to the original structure, and wears a rough road to and from his dwelling. He does little more than fish and chop wood. Even when he is very old, I can depend upon hearing at twilight a steady and slow *thwank, thwank, thwank* from his axe as he splits wood. If he suspects my nearby presence, he does not acknowledge me. When the bittersweet vines flash their stony orange notes, he again closes his front door and leaves.

During his seasonal absences, I sometimes steal into the dwelling. Mounted upon the door is a brass knocker shaped like a fist. I lift and drop the knocker just to hear it. The inside of the dwelling is rough and unfinished; one large open room is furnished with a palette, a chair near the fireplace, a table with a large metal tub, and open shelves for food and a few bowls, cups, and pans. In another room, books fill a wall of shelves. Sometimes I take a jar of meal or a pouch of dried fruit. But more sustaining to me than the rations are the old man's books. Year by year, I make my way through each volume and refine my understanding of the words. My winter days are filled with Aesop's *Fables*, later *The Iliad*, eventually Mary Shelley's *Frankenstein*, later still Emile Zola's *Paris*. A few of them I keep with me in my den. It is through the old man's library that I come to read *Beowulf*, horrified by the poet's description of my people.

I take a thick stack of paper from a shelf, a jar of ink, and a black-stained, metal-nibbed stylus. Upon several sheets, I write a long letter to the old man telling the true story, and leave it upon the large table tucked beneath the cover of the fictionalized account. I take the paper, ink, and stylus with me back to my den; the paper is smoother than any vellum, the ink perfectly black, and the stylus more comfortably balanced for writing than any bone or quill.

I expect the old man to return. The daily portion of sunlight lengthens. Tender ferns uncurl from the ground. Grubs stir and roll in abundant gray and plump white clusters beneath each rock. I feast upon these spring offerings and cheer myself with thoughts that the quiet old man of books will read my letter and understand. Even welcome me.

The warm months slip away, then leafy trees blush scarlet, and soon it is winter. As winter passes I reread the last book of the collection and eat the last jar of preserved fruit. The next spring he still does not return.

* * *

A team of horses and wagon lumber up the rough road to the cabin. From a safe distance and well hidden in the shadows of the ravine, I watch two men enter the cabin and emerge bearing the furniture, armloads of books, and robes. They heap it all together in a clearing just to the side of the porch. When they finish, one takes a jug from the wagon, pours its contents over the pile and sets it afire. I almost wail as I watch, horrified, while the book covers smoke into flame and fragile scraps of paper turn into light pieces of ash, some of which lift and float through the air in my direction. As the men speak, I catch fragments of their peppery conversation—*such old shat, what a smell, who reads this junk, nothing but mildewed pages.* The fire consumes each volume, each scrap of other worlds, as the men stand and talk, sharing drink from a large bottle. By twilight the contents of the cabin are reduced to a few charred leather covers and a pile of paper ash. From the creek, the men draw a few buckets of water and douse the remains. They climb into the wagon and drive away. In horror I run to the cabin and fling open the door, its fist-shaped door knocker rattling. Inside, I find the room cleared. Only the wood table and chair, the tub, and empty shelves remain.

* * *

Soon after, you arrive.

During a magenta-charged sunset, I hear wagon wheels echoing among the leafing birches. A horse and wagon appear. I crouch out of sight and watch you climb down from the wagon—a man, woman and small girl.

The man goes into the cabin and emerges, shouting, "Cleared out just as I asked. It is all ours now."

You walk around the cabin, murmur to each other in soft voices, and then carry several trunks inside. The next morning I watch the door burst

"Ruthie, don't go too far. Stay near the cabin."

"Yes, Mama." You turn and bound back up the step to hug Mama standing at the open door.

You run into the woods until you come quite near me. You stop, your breath high in your chest. I can see the pulse at your neck. You smell like fresh moss, and your thoughts race beyond my ability to read them. Nothing evil or mean-spirited issues from your being. Goodness drifts from you with every step and gesture. You run a little further from the cabin and come to stand a few steps away from my dwelling place. Like a deer, you lift your head and sniff at the air, and then you turn and look in the direction of where I sit holding my breath. I do not believe you see me, but you lean toward where I am as if trying fix your eyes upon me.

"Ruthie! Ruth Anna Gilbert, where are you?"

You run like sunlight to your mother.

"Evelyn, you need to get control over that girl." When you hear the thunder voice of your father, you pull back on your mother's hand.

"Come now, sweetheart. Time for lunch. We want to keep your father in good temper now, don't we?"

One afternoon, you nearly come into my den. Awakening from sleep, my vision is blurry, and I think some small deer has wandered near the opening to my den. Then I smell your quiet fragrance, like fresh clover, and know it is not a forest animal. I can hear your heart thrumming like a house wren's. I can taste your fear. Do you see the glow from my eyes? You do not grimace, flinch, or tremble.

I want to answer your call, but do not breathe. I close my eyes, and when I open them again, you turn and run back toward the cabin.

* * *

I watch you with your mother. Your beauty increases daily. I never expected to feel such warmth toward a Smallheaded again. And now, in this far place of my life, I am struck with a sympathy similar to, yet gentler, than what I felt for Brother Cloaved, the sisters, Galambos, Tambor, and the Akkara.

I do not trust the man. Your mother calls him Silas. He offers you nothing but neglect and disregard. He leaves the two of you for weeks at a time. As I watch you, I realize Evelyn stands taller when he is gone. When Silas is away, the two of you laugh with ease, play games of chase, and sing songs where cider rhymes with spider.

* * *

Evelyn tells you to never venture far from the cabin. But as you grow more comfortable with the woods, you grow more adventuresome. You are attracted to the small clearing near my den, where sunlight gathers and the long stem grasses grow dense and lush. Hoisting your basket, you often come to sing and play with a small figurine that wears a dress that matches yours. I keep well hidden from sight. Few things are as beautiful as a child engaged in the realm of her imagination, lost to any sense of herself, at an age where danger or evil is not even a passing thought.

You dance with the long-skirted grass dolls you fashion. For them, you build a many-turreted castle from strips of moss and carefully stripped twigs. You write long, elaborate stories on scrolls made from brown wrapping paper and strips of willow. You try to fly upon wings of gathered tamarack boughs.

I find myself creeping closer and closer to the opening of my cave, and then beyond that, sneaking nearer to you within the cover of the tall grass. If you turn toward me, I become motionless. Sometimes you peer through the gloaming where I hide and sway silent and breathless, until you turn back to your play. Then you saunter back to the cabin— back to your mother—and lunch of noodle soup and wild blueberry jam on bread. Moved by my curiosity, I ease close to the cabin at night and crouch below an open window, and hear you speak of me to Evelyn. You are at dinner. I can hear your cutlery knock against plates and can smell the buttery fried eggs and crusty cornbread.

"You have such an imagination. Such a story. Nothing lives in the cave."

"No, Momma. It is true. I think there is a troll in the cave."

Evelyn laughs with a voice of flute notes.

"Let us walk there this evening and go and see just what is there."

"Oh no, Momma. We must not. I think the troll is a nice creature who is scared of us."

"Then should you not also leave her—it—alone?"

"Someday she won't be afraid of me, and she will come out to play and become friends. But I will wait for her to be ready."

I hear the clatter of plates being gathered.

"Just be careful, my darling. Be safe and always come home to me."

"Of course, Momma. When will Pappa be back?"

"I don't know, dearest. When he has hunted enough, I imagine."

"I like it best when it is just the two of us. The two of us and the troll in the cave."

"I tell you, dearest, there are no such things as trolls."

"Maybe an elf then?"

"No elves, either, Ruthie."

"It is true I have not seen her. But I know she's there."

"And just how is it you know it's a she?"

The two of them laugh. Their laughs are strikingly similar, low and high ripples of each other.

"I think I'll take her a treat tomorrow. I just know it's a she."

I realize I am smiling as I turn from the window and return to my den. The next morning, I find a plate of oat biscuits at the entrance of my dwelling. I do not touch them, although I want to.

You persist in gifting gestures. I find a small, linen-covered basket at my den's entrance, and from it I eat ginger cake and drink the Kerr jar of lukewarm tea, saving the soft cheese and smoked fish for later. That night, I set the empty basket at the cabin's back door, the cloth folded into a careful square.

A few days pass, and the basket is left again. I savor the thick slices of brown bread lathered with fresh butter. This time I put a small amulet of amber inside the basket and set it back where you left it. Every fortnight or so, you leave a basket with some seasonal treat for me—slices of smoked venison, a small cake dense with dates, a berry tart. I return the favors with small keepsakes of things I make—a reed flute, soft birch carved into a knot-linked puzzle, a perfectly round river stone.

* * *

My dreams fill with amethyst colors, the rushing sound of my own heartbeat, long and turning pathways—not tunnels leading to nowhere, but to the Labyrinth. Yes, at last. The images and guides from the stones of the Labyrinth find me here. It is as if I am seated within its glittering walls again; I dwell again in the time of peace for my tribe. I hear the old songs, the long measure of prayers and incantations.

In these dreams, I teach them to you, Ruthie. And with each gift of memory comes an easing of the tightness in my joints. I do not fear the increasing weakness of my body; it will not be able to contain my spirit for much longer. But now I will be able to offer up to death not a broken spirit, but one that is invigorated and revitalized.

* * *

Silas returns. In the cover of darkness, I go to the cabin and listen and watch. My sense of him is keen. After you sleep, and I can feel the peace of your dreaming breath, I hear him beating Evelyn. She does not cry out. But I can smell her tears.

I am relieved when at last he leaves again. After he rides out of sight, the two of you burst out of the cabin with arms wide, welcoming the day of liberation. All day you wander through the hills; I follow at a safe and undetected distance. You find where the wild asparagus grows and stumble upon the thickest spreads of watercress. You wade into the cool springs. You build a fire near the lake, pierce a trout you catch with a stick and roast it. You sing a song full of nonsense about cloud hugs and biscuit waterfalls; Evelyn dances along to your song, and she does not stop smiling for the rest of the day. It is nearly dark by the time you make your way back to the cabin, and there I silently bid you sweet slumber.

I hear music from the flute I left in the basket. I look out from my den and watch you as you hold the flute against your lips and dance your fingers over the holes. Soon you make the flute moan like the wind through the red pine, trill like the red-winged black birds, gruff like the soft-chested grouse. I wonder how you have explained the instrument's appearance to Evelyn. It is old, its patina a mottled gray and umber. I expect Evelyn rationalizes it as something uncovered by the rain, as she well could have with the other gifts. Or that a hungry animal empties the contents of the baskets you insist upon taking to your friendly forest troll.

You do not go beyond the threshold to my den. I believe you prefer to imagine what I am and remain content with those possibilities.

In the basket you have left a lamp filled with citrus-scented oil and a box of small sticks that flame when scraped against my flint. The glow from the lamp is more intense than that offered by the fat and tallow I use. The wick burns clean, unlike the twisted hemp I fashion for my need. My eyes do not water from the lamp's smoke.

Well near the end of summer, I walk into the clear night and hear my wolves. They are fat and joyful. Their pups are doing well; I hear them sing. They are not hungry. I turn to return to my table and see a shadow thickening and taking form near the entrance to my cave. It collects into the shape of Tambor. Tambor draws near me.

"You must deal with the malevolence of the child's father Silas. You must not stay apart. This time, you must take action before it is too late."

I am about to speak and ask what I should do, when Tambor fades and disappears. I close my eyes. The words, *"This time, you must take action before it is too late"* echo in my mind.

* * *

It may be unwise to open myself to you, Ruthie, but I am happy knowing you are near. I look forward to hearing your dulcet voice. I keep to the shadows, content to watch and wonder. In your joy I manifest my Illisante and Galambos. With each song I feel the warmth of Brother Cloaved, the joy of Sister Carmelia, and the love of Yargis. Through you I find more than ample measure of comfort. Because you are so strong and vibrant, I do not fear your being taken away from me too soon, like my other loves.

My other loves. The one ache that is changed, but undiminished. Certainly these loves are sent to me by Yargis. It is indeed only possible to feel him close when I love another. I believe he finds pleasure and some relief in that.

* * *

In a dream, Tambor appears to me in the shape of a giant dragonfly, rising up from the surface of the lake, from the center of the full moon's reflection. It flies silently to where I stand at the shore where I dry myself after an evening bath. It turns into the shape of a stag, looks at me for several moments, and then disappears. Tambor does not speak this time, but the shapes presented underscore the message, the call that I protect you.

Then Silas returns.

For several days you do not approach my den. When dark falls and the lights are lit in the cabin, I realize how dependent my heart has become upon your regular near visits.

This time Silas is even louder and more malicious. While meat he brings back from his hunt roasts on the fire for dinner, his words ricochet through the trees, sending all the small creatures into their homes. He tramps past the entrance to my den, his large feet crunching down the tender grass, pulling you along with him. I catch a glimpse of you as you pass, and you turn to peer at the entry to my home. If you could have gathered a little more courage, I think you would have bolted from him and run to me. I watch that thought form in your mind for just a moment. Then he wrenches your arm.

"Pay attention, you stupid child."

Your fear of him wipes out any thought of rebellion.

I wait until it is dark. In the moonless night, I am hooded by darkness and make my way to the cabin. Through a window I look in to see that on the floor near the fireplace are heaped several of his bags—a sign he is there for a long stay. My heart sinks. The two of you curl together in a chair. Evelyn has wrapped your wrist in bandages. You cry yourselves to sleep that night.

Somehow you slip away in the first gray reaches of dawn, and I awake to watch you approach, carrying a basket covered with a white cloth. After you leave it and run back to the cabin, I bring it in and find in it half a loaf of bread, some cheese, and several slices of crisp bacon. This time, I do not return the basket.

Evelyn's fear of Silas colors her movements in ways different than before.

I have not glided in another's dream for a long time. After leaving the Akkara, I wanted nothing to do with anyone else's dreams. When the old man lived near me, I was not curious enough to enter his realm of sleep. But now a dream with an overwhelming force fills the night, and I am compelled to enter, with great care. The images swirl in brilliant hues of red and ochre. At first, I am disoriented and cannot find the top or bottom of the dream and cast about in it as if drowning. Then I hear a muffled cry—it is yours. A deep yell follows— no, not a yell, but a howl, almost inhuman—the other side of human, primal and shrill. Silas flies like a raptor above me. He howls again and becomes larger, his head expanding, and his mouth open wide. Uncertain whether I have entered his nightmare or yours, I keep my presence unknown. If I learn it is yours, I will comfort you. If it is his, I will not want to be discovered so soon.

Dread seeps around me and I move toward a large semblance of Silas. His shape shifts and he becomes a wheel, his head the hub, multiple arms as spokes, and it begins to roll toward a stack of logs, logs of elongated women's torsos. The hands on the wheels turn into blades and Silas begins to laugh with twisted pleasure. It is his dream. I fly toward the wheel, grasp the hub, and hurl it away from the stack of women's flesh. The images vanish and I am within his mind, his thoughts confused, the dream deflated. Deciding to appear to him, I present my largest self so he can see only one part of me at a time — my face, a hand, leg. He staggers.

"Do not harm them."

He shudders and is able to gain more control of his thoughts, and I feel the dream window closing. Before leaving his dreamscape, I press into his consciousness one lasting image of me and then I disappear. I awaken, sweating.

The door to the cabin opens and slams shut. Silas' step sounds across the cabin entrance, down steps, and into the fallen leaves. At the edge of the clearing he stops, and I hear the stream of his urine, his satisfied grunt. He stands less than fifteen paces from where I crouch. The air sours with the scent of his sperm, sweat, and traces of Evelyn's blood. Bile rises in my throat. How have I not heard this last struggle? What signs did I miss? Was she becoming so adept at denying the pain? As he stands there, breathing in the night air, I catch fragments of what flashes in his mind: Evelyn's body resisting, the taste of bitter drink, a thick sock from his foot jammed down her throat, no waking the child this time—the child, so young, beautiful, untouched, not like Evelyn.

The last few images startle me. My greatest fear confirmed. A deer near the cabin springs from his nest. He bounds past Silas and toward my den, turns again, and runs deep into the woods. Silas gasps at first in fear, then he chuckles and mutters, "Too bad I don't have my rifle."

He returns to the cabin, and lantern light fills the windows of the front room. I steal to a front window and watch him take a glass and fill it from a half-filled bottle. He runs his hands through his hair, takes up the glass, gulps down all its contents, and fills it again with the last of the bottle's contents. He crosses the room and sits down in the chair nearest the fireplace. I try to find your or Evelyn's dreams, but they are dim and scant, overpowered by Silas' seething.

He leans back in the chair and drinks from his glass. After the last swallow, he looks down into the bottom of the glass and sneers at what he does not find there. Just then in the archway to their bedroom appears Evelyn, holding a cloth to her lip, her right eye swollen.

He looks at her without an apology and stands, knocking the chair over. "I leave in the morning. We will need more venison."

He pushes past her into the bedroom, and she stands motionless at the center of the front room. I want to press an open palm upon the pane and reveal myself as I watch her gentle, aching face. But she would be horrified.

Weariness washes over me. My joints ache and my mouth is dry. I slink back to my den, take a deep drink of water and swallow a few nuts, but do not taste them. I stretch out upon my sleeping pallet, wrap soft skin robes around me, and fall into a deep sleep. When I awake, it is an early afternoon. The gray sky and warm air are deepened by the maple wood smoke from the cabin's chimney.

"Momma! Momma! Come play!"

"Not right now, dear. I'm too sick."

"Then I'll take care of you. I'm the doctor, you be the patient." You rush back into the cabin.

Silas is gone. The front door of the cabin is open, and I can make out Evelyn's form stretched back upon the cushions of the large chair in the front room. You cover her with faded quilts and stroke her forehead and cheeks.

"You rest. I'll make you better."

"You should go out and play. Stay near the cabin."

"No, Momma." You are like a dove. "I will take care of you. Now, you're not being quiet. You must rest. Here, eat this first." You take a crumbling golden biscuit and with gentle fingers feed Evelyn, offering a sip of water from a red mug. I can even taste the buttery bread dissolve on my own tongue. Your brow furrows from the serious focus you give your role.

"Make me a promise." Evelyn feels sleep dragging her down into its warmth.

"Promise? A big promise? Secret promise?"

"Important promise."

"What, my precious Momma?" You brush crumbs from your mother's shirt front and tuck a muffler closer to her ear.

"Promise that if some night I come and tell you to follow me without making a sound, you will do it. Can you promise me that? I need to get stronger, so I need to rest. But promise me that. Understand, Ruthie?"

"I promise," you whisper into Evelyn's ear. "Now get better. I'll sing you into a good dream, you'll see."

I too drift upon the gentle tide of your voice and carry your song with me back to my den, where I stretch myself out into sleep:

All is sweet and full of clouds.
Clouds made of stars.
Go to sleep and you will dream.
My forest keeper will keep you safe—
my golden forest keeper.
All is fine and full of stars.

Clouds made of stars.
Go to sleep and you will dream.
My forest—my forest—
my forest keeper.

As I climb into sleep, I realize you are singing to your mother about me.

* * *

Before you arrived, I would have welcomed the dark, starkly numbing slumber that signals the arrival of the final sleep. I had even thought of hastening its dark arrival by drinking tea brewed from cedar bark and dried stalks of lupine. But now, I want to hold it off. At least a while longer. I cannot abandon you.

In the depth of my black sleep, Tambor's silhouette stands before me. "He is back. You must do something. He will soon be after the child."

"Already?" I should not need to question the obvious.

A sense of urgency and consequence mingles with the deep green scent of the woodland. "Yes. In the night. You will need to do something, and your action must be taken soon, or he will harm the child. Now, there is something deeper, unstable, and revolting. The back of the wagon is filled with jugs and bottles. He said he's here to stay. The mother Evelyn began to cry and he took the little girl Ruthie into his arms, and it was not kind." Tambor looks at me. "I am but spirit. You must act."

"I know, I know. But how and what? These last few months, I've been so weak."

"She must meet you in her dream, the mother Evelyn. Reveal yourself, assure her, and instruct her to take the child and leave. And then you must be rid of him." Tambor shakes as the words tumble upon me.

"I am sorry. Please forgive me, forgive me for thinking that by simply being near and watching, I was doing enough."

"Don't think like that. I know you would do something if it were clear he was going to harm the little one. If you were well, if you were younger, none of this would have passed without your notice. As you have thought, I am here for you, but not before you are finished with what you need to do. Protect the mother and her child."

With those words Tambor disappears, leaving me unsettled. He is right. I gather your two images into my mind, Evelyn and Ruthie, and prepare to do whatever necessary to guarantee your safety. It is easy to gain entry into Evelyn's dream. Exhaustion weaves thick through her sleep. With such weariness there is no resistance. I remain as much in the shadows of her mind as possible, wanting her to believe the dream is a benevolent vision and not a malevolent nightmare. I sing to her ancient airs and tunes from my own childhood, the evening songs of the brothers, the prayerful melodies that arose from the convent, some of the lines read until memorized from scrolls found in the Akkara's holding. I ease my own image gently into her dream and she does not protest.

"Evelyn." I take her hand and look into her eyes. She does not shrink from my touch. She returns my gaze with steady trust. "Each night, I dream for the safety and happiness of your daughter Ruthie, do you not?"

"Yes, yes, I do. Every night. Every morning. With each waking breath."

"Well, those dreams are answered. I am here to tell you what you must do. Take Ruthie and all you can carry away from here. Never return. Tomorrow night. Just make certain Silas sleeps deep and early. My plan is simple. With Silas in a drunken slumber, leave him. Take Ruthie and leave on horseback. I will keep Silas in a rich dream he will not want to leave, from which he will not awaken until well into the next day—all the time you two will need to get far ahead and away. You will go to the seaside village, and you will sell the horse, and then you will purchase passage to a place he does not know and cannot find. There you will have a new life."

I seed Evelyn's dreams with these clear images, and in the morning, her shoulders are set back with grave and formidable resolve.

* * *

Evelyn believes in what my dream message offers. I sense her comforting relief and a frequent, clear thought like a gasp: *Freedom*. She wonders why the plan hadn't been so obvious earlier.

That evening I watch through the window as she pours drink after drink for Silas, how she lulls him with enchantingly long-withheld kindnesses—a cabled muffler around his shoulders, the pipe packed with tobacco set at his elbow, another mug of steaming, spiked cider. How readily he responds, drinking all she pours until his head rests upon her breast. She eases his head down upon the table and then goes to you. As you promised, you follow Evelyn in obedient silence.

The two of you take the horse, and sensing the critical juncture you face, without a whinny, she takes you both into the night. The two of you ride away from me. Toward your own lives.

Taking guard at the cabin door, I watch Silas sleep. His dreams are a tangle of confused images: his wild game traps are oversized and glittering, crammed with human body parts caught in their jaws that move and twist, then turn into boats, cannons, and guns flowing with blood. All of Silas' horrors and demons parade through his dreams, and I cross to where he sleeps. He awakes with a cry, looks around and works to focus on my form. His mouth turns into a grimace, eyes widen into terror. He bolts up and makes for his rifle leaning near the door. In two steps I close the gap of space between us, then take him by his bony shoulders to lift him until his head touches the ceiling. He screams and yells, kicking with all his might against my chest, striking at my arms. I dangle him aloft for a few moments and then drop him. He gathers himself and runs from the cabin, and I follow. It is an easy pursuit. I intend only to scare him, and I maintain my distance of a few paces behind him as he runs to the east, where the sun begins to lick the high tamarack limbs with red-fringed light. He stumbles about in the woods as if he were in unfamiliar terrain. He looks over his shoulder at me, and I follow him steady and surefooted.

Then he drops out of sight, past the large granite boulder and circle of matching stones where, a few weeks earlier, I watched you play a game you named Castle and Islands. Silas falls over a sharp ledge and into a ravine. I stop and wait for some sound, some anguished call, but hear none. At the edge of the ravine, I look down upon Silas's body impaled by a bare and standing spruce. His body flinches and then settles into limp stillness as his spirit departs.

I consider climbing down to him, to perhaps gather him up, and later dig a grave for him in the cool forest earth. But I do not. I savor the tangible severance of his life-hold upon you. I close my eyes and chart your beating hearts, already far from here, and gaining distance with each breath I take. The cold chill of the night inches up from the ground through my feet and numbs my body. At last I turn and return to the cabin. I build a high fire in the fireplace, stretch out in front of it, and sleep.

When I awaken, I begin this chronicle, and, but for time to sleep, eat or stretch, I do not move from this task at your table.

Now I am nearly done. I lose track of time. How long has it been, Evelyn and Ruthie, since you left these woods? How long have I been scratching out these inky words? I feel weak. It is discomfiting to feel a little stronger, only to then feel my insides clutch and tear away. In the dark I cannot tell if it is the middle of the night, or just before dawn, or if whole days slip by without my noting their passage. I have no appetite for food but crave the close comfort of my den. I return to it and the remnants of my life.

EPILOGUE

1931

My name is Ruth Anna Gilbert. The story you hold in your hand I transcribed from the original manuscript, which was hidden away by its author for me to find.

It is the story of a woman named Rehsotis, a woman who survived the times of legend, of great darkness, and of tenuous illumination. She lived beyond all reason, and for longer than should be believed.

Rehsotis belonged to the Anathian, a race who once walked the earth. They listened not only to their own dreams, but to ancestor spirits murmuring their insights from the ages, to ghosts keening their visions from timeless dimensions, to deities pulling at their souls from the forests.

Speak it softly, and it seems a gentle enough name. Nearly a hum. Not much more than a deep murmur. You have probably heard of him; his story is found in *Beowulf*, the oldest surviving epic tale in English literature, first written down in Old English sometime before the tenth century. It is amazing how liquid the proportion of time can be when we look at stories from so long ago. We say *sometime* and log it a few hundred years before or a few hundred years after, nod, and say *close enough*. How sad—all those years of particulars, jumbled and swept together. So many stories lost and forgotten—a mere few enlarged and embellished.

You may see the oldest extant copy of *Beowulf* in the British Library of London, a fine place indeed for a manuscript. I went once to see it and learned that this one precious copy was part of the private library of a man named Sir Robert Bruce Cotton; a fire had nearly destroyed it, leaving the manuscript's edges charred.

Do not look within the pages of *Beowulf* to find Rehsotis. You will not find her there. You will read about Grendel, his mother, about Beowulf, dragons, and many other astounding things. But you will find nothing about Grendel's sister Rehsotis.

Her story is here.

I cannot say that I actually met Rehsotis. I sensed her in the way a young child can. My mother Evelyn, father Silas, and I lived for a short time in a remote cabin. Rehsotis dwelt in a den nearby. My encounters with her were slight glimpses—a motion between the trees, a sense of someone watching me, a mysterious exchange of gifts in a basket.

Abruptly, mother and I left the cabin. We left my father. We left Rehsotis. And then that season in the woods receded into a distant, but resonant, memory—a part of the *sometime* of childhood. As an adult, I thought of Rehsotis as someone I summoned because of my need as an only child to fill the lonely landscape. I believed that only I saw her. When I recollected these images and stories to my mother, she became unusually quiet and offered nothing in return. After a time, I stopped asking.

For years a part of me wandered, searching for the forested place of my youth. A green and golden memory of a season passed in magical isolation but tainted by the awareness of something sinister lurking therein. I dreamt of two beings I could not name but knew. One was a monster who lived within the walls of my own home. The other, a being some would call a monster, but whom I understood as protector and angel.

Until she grew old and felt an increasing obligation to reveal the truth, my mother would not speak of that season we spent in the forest. During all those years, I was drawn to my memories of the season again and again, crafting the images and sensations of that summer from the all-too-real but unreliable and mutable material of my memory. Not until she was near death did she tell me all about our time at the cabin with my father. She asked me to forgive her for not having spoken about it earlier, that she did not realize how much I needed and craved the particularities of those months. Initially she hoped that by not telling me, she would spare me from my father's cruelty. She thought by keeping me free of the details of that short and fleeting portion of my life, time would wear and pull it smoothly void and perfectly forgotten.

She spoke at last of those last nights in the woods, about the dream so clear to her; she awoke from it knowing precisely what she needed to do. She told me that during our last night in the cabin, it began to rain, and the clock seemed to mark the hours too slowly; she described for me how she marked the time with each glass of whiskey she poured for my father. In my mind I could envision us dressed and clutched tightly onto the horse, heading away in the moonlight.

Although my mother Evelyn still dismissed my sense of a woodland creature as a youthfully hopeful fantasy, I became more certain such a being had indeed existed. As Mother described our departure and flight from my father, I recalled the sense of the eyes of Rehsotis watching us leave, blessing our journey with her strong will.

After Mother told me the story, and in the weeks following her death, I dreamed I was Rehsotis—but not weary or tired as she had been at the end of her life when she wrote her chronicle. I stood next to a large boulder. Around me were other smaller boulders and stones twistingly arranged in a circle. At my feet lay the body of Silas. Bits of earth, moss, and lichen swirled and flew around me. Then in the dream, I lay down beneath the fragrant dome of balsam limbs. The balsam turned from blue to black to midnight, then to violet, and finally a deep amethyst. I awoke understanding where I needed to go, what I needed to do.

At dawn I gathered a map, shovel, linen sack, red flannel, and several linen sheets. I packed a satchel of food and filled a decanter with strong coffee. I drove my old red truck to the forests several hours north of my home.

From a knowing deeper than memory, I traced and followed the roads that took me farther into the woods, until finally I stumbled onto a logging trail hidden by vetch and clumps of sedge. I knew I was close to my past, the sense of arrival pulling me closer to what I sought. I parked the truck and brought out my supplies, along with my compass. I never needed the compass.

Without hesitation, I found my way.

The cabin was a ruin, the roof caved in, the walls covered by moss on the north side and riddled with holes drilled by bugs and woodpeckers, and the porch floor crumbled shards.

Her den was right where I knew it would be. Oh, how many times had I walked from the cabin to the arch of her dwelling space. This time I did not hesitate. This time I went in and found a space remarkably intact: A shelf of books—Plutarch, the Bible, Chaucer, Shakespeare, Dickinson. Leather pouches filled with seeds, dried berries, bark, thick rosins hanging from hooks on the wall. A low table arranged with two stoneware bowls, several carved wooden spoons, a pink seashell, a small amber-topped box. And this volume. Swaddled in tapestry faded into fragility, inches of thick yellow pages bound between suede covers and wrapped in a leather cord. Across the pages flowed an even script, full of embellishments yet easily readable, for I was much accustomed to ancient texts after years of study. I carried it out into the sunlight and stretched out on the deep grass.

I read it all—then and there—and found my way back into my childhood. I found a good many other things.

All story distills to one essential conflict: strength versus strength. This story is no different. Love versus hate. Time versus memory. Hope versus despair. At the entrance to her den, the sun warmed my limbs, the clear forest air moved soft in my lungs. When I finished, I went back into her dwelling.

Along the back wall stretched the sleeping pallet heaped with leather hides. Gently I lifted away the crumbling coverings and exposed the remains of Rehsotis. The burning glass gleamed in the place where her heart had been.

I could feel her. Rehsotis' spirit rose up and stood next to me. She took my hand and held it tightly. We listened to the sounds of the forest in autumn drifting to us on a cedar and white-pine fanned breeze—piping finches, shushing aspen leaves, nattering squirrels. Then I silently gathered Rehsotis' remains into the linen sack.

I thought of keeping the burning glass. I found it more beautiful than she described. Even in the dim light of the den, the thin, multi-sided gemstone glowed with a life of its own along its edges and down to a fine, radiant point. But it belonged with her. The heat of its touch lingered long in my palm.

I believe she watched me.

It saddened me to think about how alone Rehsotis had been. I thought about this world we Smallheaded think we have mastered, and knew the depth of our ignorance, the shame of our folly.

From what she wrote of her confrontation with Silas, I recreated her steps. I closed my eyes and divined where she had stepped into the woods some thirty years before. I walked for about an hour, marking my way through the woods with red strips of felt. I was just starting to second-guess myself, thinking it was all a ridiculous error in judgment, when I came upon the lichen-mottled boulder and mossy circle of stones from my dream. I found the opening in the outermost ring and entered to walk the space between the stones, back and around, left and right, near and far, until I came to the center and rested my hand on the boulder. I took longer walking my way out of the labyrinth. When I finally exited, I walked just beyond the circle of stones and looked down into a ravine. Certainly, the wear of years and the attendant rain and wind moved the edge of the ledge, shifting the contours of the ravine. But I knew I surveyed the final resting place of my father Silas. I did not need to climb down and look for his remains. I knew they were there and I did not want to claim them.

I stumbled back to the clearing following the small red flags—startling in their brightness against the luminous birch trees. I sat again for a long time outside the den. Then I took the large linen sack filled with her remains and wrapped it all in a sheet I could sling over my back. I hiked out to the logging road, eased the bundle onto the seat next to me, and took the winding roads back home.

That night I reread her story. In the morning, fueled by a pot of hot coffee, I opened my journal to a blank page and drew a labyrinth. While letting my recollections of Rehsotis guide my pen around the page, what was once dismissed as only the caricatured fantasies of a child gained the dimensions of flesh and shadows of breath.

In the pre-dawn, with the sketch, herbs gathered from my garden, and Rehsotis' remains, I drove to the seacoast and arrived at sunrise. Alone on the beach, I stripped off my shoes and stockings and spent the day on my knees spading my labyrinth deep and large into the tide-evened sand. At dusk, I gathered dry driftwood, heaped it at the labyrinth's center, and set it on fire. With linen cord, I bound her remains with thick sprays of sage and rosemary and carried the bundle like an infant into the labyrinth. Upon reaching its center, I rested my offering upon the compact pyre of wood and lit a fire. Like a scarf, smoke unfurled into the dawn-soft breeze and drifted east toward the far-glittering surface of the sea. At my feet, the fire burned steadily, and I fed more driftwood to its scarlet tongues throughout the day. Later, the returning tide softened the sand mounds of my reconceived Labyrinth of the Tribe of Anath. The ashy remains of Rehsotis—bits of salt and crumbled bones—swirled around and against me as the seawater rose to my waist. When moonlight washed the beach blue, I heard Rehsotis singing.

Enveloped by her sighing spirit, I whispered, "Rest easy, dear Rehsotis. Daughter of Yenheth. Sister of Grendel. Protector. Sage. Shaman. My Forest Guardian. I will never forget you."

ACKNOWLEDGMENTS

I am filled with gratitude for the many who have been a part of my journey to bring this work to the page: Abby Werlock, for connecting me to Diana Finch, who has believed in the magic of this tale from its beginning. Those who took the time to read parts or the whole of it, who nodded in the affirmative to my explanations, and who offered words of encouragement: Ilene Dawn Alexander, Nancy Antenucci, Judy Yates Borger, Mary Carlsen, Dennis Cass, Karen Cherewatuk, Anna Christophorides, Tim Clausen, Marly Cornell, Marian Deegan, Mary Moore Easter, Anastasia Faunce, Susan Foster, Lynne Franklin, Geordie Griffiths, Michael Hamerski, Shoonie Hartwig, Katherine Woodburn Hirsh, Mary Hughes, Neal Karlen, Tracy Karner, Judith Katz, Deborah Keenan, Paul Krubick, Sigi Leonhard, Mary Logue, JoAnne Makela, Joe Manion, Mary Jane Manion, Yann Martel, Maree Merriam, Kit Naylor, Riki Kölbl Nelson, Joan Nygren, Therese Pautz, Sherry Roberts, Karen Rue, Karen Sandburg, Faith Sullivan, Mary Titus, Kim Todd, Cynthia Uhrich, Ozlem Ursen, Dawn Vogel, Beverly Voldseth, Karen Herseth Wee. For the careful attention to each word, my forever-gratitude to Stevie Beck and Cassidy Swanson, and the full-court team at Calumet Editions. And most especially my children Madeleine and Samuel, for always asking for another story.

ABOUT THE AUTHOR

Award-winning writer Susan Thurston has published extensively with work in the *Minneapolis Star Tribune, Los Angeles Review, The Writer's Almanac with Garrison Keillor, Low Down and Coming On* (Red Dragonfly Press), *Tremors Vibrations Enough to Rearrange the World* (Heywood Press), *Upon Arrival of Illness* (Savage Press), *Poetry Quarterly*, the cookbook *Cooking Up the Good Life* (University of Minnesota Press), and the chapbook *Wild Bone Season* (Heywood Press)

The haunting language of Beowulf always entranced Thurston and she immediately identified with the invaded: Grendel and his mother. Drawing upon those impressions and boundless research about legends and myth, she created Sister of Grendel, her first published novel.

Thurston has earned her living by her pen and is a tireless educator and communicator about the power of story. She relishes exploring the remnants that birth legends, from Bronze Age jewelry discovered in English sod to ancient gnarled orchards abandoned on Greek islands. She lives in St. Paul, Minnesota.